Allen Cortez assisted Dr. Eichbaum as he made the initial incisions, lifting away the flesh of the scalp and, referring to the images of a CAT-scan on an overhead monitor, sawed a fragment of the man's skull away, revealing the brain within. It was swollen and strangely discolored, appearing dark and bruised.

"This is odd," stated the neurosurgeon. "Very odd indeed."

Allen said nothing. To him, it wasn't very odd at all. He leaned forward, examining the wrinkled folds of the patient's discolored cerebrum.

"What are you looking for, Allen?" Eldan asked him after a moment.

"*That*," he said.

He could tell that Dr. Eichbaum was startled by the discovery he had made. Clinging to the tissue of the brain was not one blue black spider, but three. They seemed to pulsate, as though feeding off the circulation of the cranial organ. But, no, on further inspection, Allen surmised that the opposite was taking place. Somehow, the spiders were delivering rather than taking, as though pumping minute amounts of some dark and nasty poison into the man's diseased brain.

THE WEB OF
LA SANGUINAIRE
And Other Arachnid Horrors

RONALD KELLY

Copyright Information

Dedication

For Scott Magill and Donald Belcher

Comrades-in-arms & partners-in-crime

Mrs. Hart's Creative Writing Class

1976-1977

Contents

Introduction 1

The Web of La Sanguinaire 4

The Memory Eater 12

Housewarming 38

Atomic Arachnid Armageddon! 48

Cell Number Nine 55

The Creeping Sands 78

Hugs and Kisses 102

Come See Spider Cave! 117

Contents

Introduction

S piders! Why did it have to be spiders?

Yeah, I know... there is one of two ways you could feel about the creepy, eight-legged critters. You could fear and loathe them the same way Indiana Jones feels about snakes in the deep, dark pit of the Well of Souls. You could totally freak out and throw shoes at them as they creep across the wall (or, in my case, a twenty-pound dumbbell, which nearly put a hole in the floor of the apartment I was living in at the time), or you could totally avoid that section of your flower bed where a gargantuan yellow garden spider has spun a window-sized web, leaving that particular patch to the mercy of weeds because of your paralyzing Arachnophobia.

On the other hand, you could be the kind who absolutely *loves* spiders. Someone who finds a big, hairy tarantula in the palm of their hand to be more soft and cuddly than horror-inducing. Maybe even one of those weirdos who doesn't mind if one crawls across their face and even—heaven forbid!—climbs inside their *mouth*. If you have watched enough Tik Tok and YouTube videos, then you know the sort of folks that I'm talking about.

So, where do I stand? Without doubt, I am of the former persuasion. Arachnids are part of my own personal Holy Terror Trinity of Creepy Crawlers: spiders, snakes, and wasps. The three totally terrorize me. If you have read my short fiction before, you know that I tend to explore the horror of spiders and snakes from time to time. Even my novel, *Fear*, has the dreaded Snake-Critter as its main antagonist. Last summer, a baby chicken snake crawled through an air conditioner vent and got stuck to a glue trap in my daughter's bedroom closet. Needless to say, I was ready to sell the house, furniture and all, and move off to Ireland, where there are no snakes (or is that just a myth?). Wasps, especially Satan's evil stepchild, the Southern red wasp (or *waspers*, as we tend to call them down here) will make me flee for my life or even run headlong into a wall trying to get away from one if it gets inside the house and starts dive-bombing my head.

However, spiders are what really mortify me the most. Much of my anxiety over the little eight-legged freaks come from two incidents during my childhood. First, a large wolf spider—a *hopping* wolf spider, no less—chased me and my cousins across a leafy, autumn back yard once when I was six-years-old. Secondly, my brother and I would sit in our garage as children, playing with our backs against the cool cinderblock wall in the sweltering heat of summer. There was a long strip of tarpaper between the blocks and the drywall that hadn't been cut away when the house had been built. After playing beneath it all summer, our father cut the tarpaper away and discovered a nest of black widow spiders living underneath. Even at the young age of eight, the idea of one of the deadly poisonous spiders dropping down the collar of my shirt horrified me to no end!

In *The Web of La Sanguinaire & Other Arachnid Horrors*, I have assembled eight tales that will make you shudder and cringe… the way you do when you feel—or *think* you feel—some unseen creature crawl across your bare legs beneath the bedcovers in the dead of night. A couple of these are oldies from my small press horror magazine days of the late 1980s. Two more appeared in other collections and four are completely original to this book.

Introduction

Several of my loyal readers have already informed me that they will *not* be indulging in this collection because of their nearly debilitating phobia of arachnids. To them I say, this is only a book of spooky stories... it is not a box of skittering, scurrying spiders that will scamper out and cover you from head to toe, as you flail and shriek in terror.

And, what about you? Do you dare take the midnight boat ride into the darkest reaches of the bayou, where the dreaded La Sanguinaire of Cajun legend spin their massive webs? Or, enter a house infested with brown recluses that are strangely hidden from sight? Maybe even enter an abandoned Texas jail where eight-legged evil has been unleashed after a long sleep in amber stone... or camp on an Australian beach, where sea spiders protect a golden treasure in the Coral Sea with a ravenous vengeance?

If so, I hope you enjoy these tales of spiders with sinister intentions. But, just remember... if the letters on the page begin to squiggle and squirm, and skitter frantically about, just tell yourself "It's only my imagination... it's only my imagination..."

Ronald Kelly
Brush Creek, Tennessee
January 2021

The Web of La Sanguinaire

L arousse would not take him there at first.

"It not safe to travel de swamp at night," the old Cajun warned in his heavy French accent.

But Douglas Scott Price was accustomed to having his own way. An extra hundred dollars laid across the old man's leathery palm soon changed his tune.

The last rays of daylight played through the Spanish moss hanging from ancient cypress trees when the two climbed into Henri Larousse's pirogue, a canoe-like boat used by many of the trappers and fishermen in the area. "What's that for?" Price asked his guide when a double-barreled shotgun was laid across the center seat.

The elderly man shrugged. "De gators, dey would rather eat than sleep. Where we are going, dey be plenty of dem."

They began their long journey into the Louisiana bayou in silence. Price sat at the bow of the boat as Larousse rowed. Deeper into the swamp they drifted and deeper did the shadows gather, until the Coleman lantern next to the scattergun had to be lit. It cast an orange glow upon the two men. The lack of conversation was awkward, but they really had nothing to talk about. The only link between them was purely monetary.

A loon screamed off in the darkness, causing the young man to jump. The elder man chuckled softly and continued to row with slow, even strokes.

"So, what is it you do for a living?" the Cajun asked. Without conscious thought, he maneuvered the dugout across the dark waters, missing exposed roots and sandbars by mere inches.

"Oh, as little as possible, really," Price replied with an air of pomposity. "I was born into old family money. Ever heard of the New England Prices? No? Well, I expected as much. Being independently wealthy tends to mean a lot of free time, but I manage to keep myself busy."

Larousse had a good idea what sort of luxuries occupied Doug Price's time. Ferraris, eighty-foot yachts, and million-dollar thoroughbreds; a wet bar always at hand and a beautiful woman waiting at every point of the compass. Larousse knew his mind as well as he knew his own. Men of wealth and influence… you could almost smell the good fortune exude from them like the odor of some cheap cologne. The Cajun had been born in backwater poverty and had lived that meager life for nearly eighty years. He could sense a rich man a mile away, like a bluetick hound catching the scent of swamp coon upon a midnight breeze.

Seeing Larousse's amused eyes in the glow of the lamp, the young man continued. "Despite what you think, old man, I do not spend every waking hour jet-setting with a buxom blonde on my knee and a martini in my hand. No, actually my interests are quite respectable. My passion has always leaned toward the biological sciences, most particularly zoology. I've contributed millions to various zoological societies; the Smithsonian, the Audubon, the Sierra. I've also devoted much of my time. I've traveled the world over collecting rare species of bird, mammal, and insect life, both for public exhibition and for my own private collection."

"And so dat be de reason we are here, rowing through the bayou at such an ungodly hour?" asked the guide. "To collect something or other?"

"Yes," said Price, a little peeved. "But don't complain. You're being well paid for this little foray. In an hour or so, you'll be back at your humble swamp shanty, stuffing that three hundred inside your mattress. And I'll leave this godforsaken place with what I came here to find."

"And that would be de creature you mentioned before?"

"That's correct," said Price. "A rare species of the order Araneae. The pronunciation of its Latin nomenclature would likely be way over your head, old man, so I won't even bother. Needless to say, the common name of the arachnid is the striped swamp spider. It has a pale underbelly, the upper shell pitch black with broad streaks of crimson on the hind section. I do hope this isn't a wild goose chase you're taking me on. You are sure that you've seen such a spider in these parts?"

Larousse nodded. "Oui, a very large and ugly thing. But only at night… never in light of day."

"Yes, they are nocturnal in nature," agreed the collector. "And they are rather large; the size of a man's fist, or so I've heard. That is why I came prepared." He patted a ten-gallon aquarium at his feet.

The darkness grew thicker, the night sounds more varied, more mysterious to one unaccustomed to the swamps. They rounded a sharp bend between two waterlogged stands of old cypress and came upon a tangle of heavy cobwebs, stretching from one side of the channel to the other. Price directed the beam of a flashlight upon the vast webs, the glow etching each silver strand upon the darkness beyond. Fat-bodied spiders the size of golf balls scuttled away from the silken centers, away from the probing light.

"Hoo-boy!" exclaimed the Cajun. He watched the long-legged things climb swiftly upward into the obscurity of the dark limbs above. "Dere be you some spiders, Mr. Price. Plenty o' them. Oughta take a bucketful back with you."

The young man seemed disinterested. "Common water spiders." He tore away the fragile network of webs with a swing of his arm and they continued on. "They've been an item of my arachnid collection for years. It is the swamp spider I'm looking for now."

They moved on into the bayou, into far reaches where the boldest of poachers dared not come, even in broad daylight. The roar of a bull gator rumbled to their left, but it was too far away to present any immediate danger.

"De thing you seek… de swamp spider… it has an interesting history, it do," Larousse said. The glow of the kerosene lamp highlighted every little wrinkle, every line and liver spot on his aged face. "Some of de Cajun people, dey still believe in de old ways, de magic and de beliefs of dere ancestors. When de French first settled de bayou, dey believed in such things. De spider of which you search, dey called it *La Sanguinaire*, "The Bloodthirsty", for it was said to be big enough to catch and devour prey larger than other insects. Birds, rabbits, dere was even a case of one trapping a wild boar in its awesome web. Some, dey say, dat even a man would fall prey every now and again, and de Sanguinaire would crawl down out of de trees and drain him of his blood. Many thought, and still do, dat dey are de souls of de damned left upon earth as punishment, left as things repulsive to be loathed by man. Some think dat dey possess magical powers… dat if a man be bitten upon de crown of de head by a Sanguinaire, he is subject to dere very wishes for de remainder of his life… to watch over dem, to protect, to provide food, if it be necessary."

Douglas Price laughed out loud at the old man's story. "And do you, old timer…" he asked with a grin, "believe these stories of the Sanguinaire?"

"I do not so much believe or disbelieve, as I respect dem. Dere be many things, Mr. Price, that are unknown to us… many strange and awful things. If you are to travel in strange lands and deal with strange people, you would do well to learn to respect local customs and not scoff so easily."

"Enough of this mumbo jumbo," said Price. "Back to the business at hand." He flashed his light upon the trunks of the cypress trees along the heavy thicket that grew dense on the mossy banks. The wide swath of light swept the shallow bank to the right, then settled there. Movement came from the shadows between a clump of gnarled, exposed roots. "Take me over there! Quickly, man, before they get away!"

Larousse steered the pirogue to the far bank as his passenger prepared the glass tank. Price slipped on a pair of heavy, rawhide gloves and, when they reached the tangle of roots, handed the flashlight to the old man. "Shine the light on that opening there," he indicated. The old man nodded sourly, thinking that the whole situation was somewhat ridiculous. All this fuss for a stupid spider! But he remembered the trio of hundred-dollar bills tucked in the pocket of his goosedown vest and did as he was told.

The pale light revealed an entire nest of the spiders, great and bulky, glistening black with streaks the color of freshly-let blood crossing their hindquarters. They tried to escape into the webbed tunnels they had constructed beneath the shelter of the cypress roots, but Price quickly dispatched two of the larger ones, placing their writhing bodies into the aquarium and clamping on the screened lid.

"Good Lord!" breathed the young man, his face livid with excitement. "Will you look at the size of these things? They're three times larger than the common tarantula." The two swamp spiders clawed at the glass walls, fairly the size of full-grown tree squirrels.

The Web of La Sanguinaire

The Cajun laughed, his broad grin showing off raw gums and a few tobacco-stained teeth. "Aw, I have seen much larger than those," he said, handing the flashlight back to its owner.

Price stared at the old gentleman, unable to determine whether the swamper was serious or just pulling his leg. He studied the two monstrous specimens in the glow of the Coleman, then glanced at his Rolex. It was a quarter after nine. "You get us back to town by midnight, old-timer, and I'll up your fee by another two hundred. Fair enough?"

Larousse nodded, his eyes hidden in the shadow of his oily fishing cap. "Oui, Monsieur Price. That would be most generous." He began to guide the low boat back into the channel from which they came.

For hours they traveled the labyrinth of channels that made up the stillwater bayou. For some reason the night sounds that had seemed so prominent before were now oddly absent. Price was aware of this, as well as the unfamiliarity of the swamp they now cruised; a swamp more densely overgrown than the one they had set into earlier in the evening. He wanted to mention the fact openly several times, but the elderly guide seemed so confident in his navigation that Price had let it go. *Probably just a shortcut back to the settlement*, he concluded. *For an extra two hundred, I bet the old geezer could find a shortcut clear to the gulf from here.*

Once, a curious gator crossed the dark waters and slammed his blunt snout against the side of the pirogue. The impact caused the lantern to topple off the center seat and over the side with a splash. When Price asked him why he hadn't fished it out, Larousse only smiled. "I can afford to lose a lantern. I have lost many to de swamp. But I can't afford to lose an arm. Look."

Price understood when he directed his flash upon the channel and saw half a dozen hungry gators floating like logs to either side of the boat.

They moved onward down the winding channel. The young collector was gradually aware that the darkness around them had thickened. The full moon that had hung overhead was gone, obscured by overlapping branches, heavy mats of Spanish moss… and something else.

He directed his beam ahead of them. A velvet wall of light mist choked the inlet a few yards ahead. "Looks as though a fog has rolled in," he said, gathering his jacket closer around him.

"Oui," replied the Cajun. "De fog… it gets as thick as gumbo in de bayou. So thick, in fact, that you can reach out and grab a fistful of it, if you so wish." His passenger shook his head skeptically at the old man's tale. "Really, monsieur. Go ahead and give it a try."

They were upon a wall of white mist now and, just to show the old man how idiotic his idea was, Price thrust his hand over the bow. His smug expression melted into confusion as his hand sank into something unsolid, yet of definite substance. It was sticky and clinging and, when he attempted to pull his hand away, found that he could not.

"Something has a hold of me, old man," he gasped. He batted at the adhesive strands with the aluminum flashlight, but it too became entangled. It dangled in the silky wall, despite its weight. "Help me, Larousse! Dammit, man, get me out of this confounded mess!"

Then he felt the distinct sensation of the boat sliding out from underneath him and realized that it actually was. With a curse, he lost his balance as he attempted to stand up and his entire weight lurched backward into the wall of unyielding mist. He was overcome with sudden terror when he realized that his body was now suspended over the dark water. He craned his head around and saw Larousse rowing the pirogue away from him, maneuvering to head back the way they had come.

"Where the hell are you going?" Douglas Price screamed, his anger quickly passing into blind panic. "Come back here this instant! I'm paying you good money, do you hear me?" He struggled wildly against the gummy strands, attempting to pull away. But he only managed to entangle himself more firmly amid the great web.

He watched as Henri Larousse began to row back up the channel. The flashlight bobbed crazily in its suspension, throwing light upon the retreating boat.

Larousse totally ignored Price's pleas for help. He didn't even turn around. He absently removed his cap to scratch his balding head.

The shimmering glow of the battery-generated light revealed two deep indentations on the back of the old man's skull. Two ugly marks that seemed to sink clear past the bone to the brain, yet that had healed over many years ago.

Douglas Scott Price screamed loudly and fought furiously with the spiral of viscid silk that imprisoned him. But, of course, there was no escape. As the darkness swallowed the old Cajun and his boat, Price was keenly aware of movement in the trees above. When he finally saw the things creeping down the web toward him, as big as pit-bull terriers, his mind snapped and he began to shriek madly.

"Bon Appetite," called Old Larousse from out of the night.

But the young man was beyond hearing him. Only the Sanguinaire acknowledged his well wishes, before they resumed their feeding.

The Memory Eater

Jay Maher was passing the dining room table, when he spotted a packet of photographs lying there. Curious, he opened the envelope and studied the twenty-four pictures that were nestled inside.

They were of a family picnic in a local park; him, his wife, Kimberly, his sixteen-year-old daughter, Katie, and their newborn daughter, Charlotte. Sitting beneath a shade tree, feasting on chicken salad sandwiches and potato chips, laughing, cutting up, and enjoying one another.

It was idyllic, except for one thing.

Jay remembered none of it.

"Kim, sweetheart," he called out. "What are these pictures?"

His wife, blonde and freckled, peeked through the doorway from where she stood at a kitchen counter, preparing dinner. "It's from our picnic, silly," she told him.

"*What* picnic?" he said, feeling his heart race a bit.

Kim looked at him as though he had suddenly grown two heads. "Our picnic last weekend, at Progressive Park."

Jay knew where the park was... just across the street from Odessa Regional Medical Center. He recalled him and Kim planning a picnic there, but he had been so busy in his new position as medical director of a new women's and children's hospital in the

The Memory Eater

Texas city, as well as unpacking at their new home in the suburb of Gardendale, that they hadn't found the time to make it a reality yet.

Or had they?

"What day was this?" he asked.

"Last Sunday afternoon," his wife said, seeming a bit annoyed. "We had lunch near the playground. Remember, we joked that Katie was too old to play on the swings and Charlotte was too young?"

Jay felt a cold sensation run through him; a mixture of confusion and fear. "No," he admitted, knowing what a fool he sounded like. "I don't remember it. Not at all."

Kim left the kitchen and appeared in the doorway, wiping her hands on a dishtowel. The expression on her pretty face was a cross between irritation and worry. "What do you mean... you don't remember it?"

Jay sat down heavily in one of the dining room chairs, still holding the photos in his hand. "I... I just *don't*. Sure, this is us in these pictures, but I have no recollection of this ever happening." A frightened look crossed his face. "Come to think of it, I don't remember anything that happened on Sunday at all."

The severe expression on his wife's face softened and she walked over and sat in a chair next to him. "You've been under so much stress lately, what with the new job and the move; it isn't a wonder that the past couple of weeks aren't just one big blur of events."

"It's not that," he told her firmly. "I don't remember any of it." He shook his head. "You know how forgetful I've been lately. But you just don't forget an entire day in your life, from the moment you wake to the moment you fall asleep." He felt something like a cold stone in the pit of his stomach. "You don't think it could possibly be... ?"

Kim knew exactly what he was about to say. She lifted a finger and pressed it against his lips, silencing him. "No, dear. Please, let's don't get into this again. You're too young to even think of having…"

"Alzheimer's?" Just uttering the word sent a spike of terror through his heart. The degenerative mental disease was one of the worst fears of his adult life, with spiders coming in at second place. He was horrified of slowly losing his mental faculties to the point of becoming a burden to his family and being robbed of his personality and identity in the process. Several months ago, it had only been one of those irrational fears that men suffered at the onset of middle-age, but his recent rash of forgetfulness and now this total elimination of a cherished memory, brought those concerns back to light.

Kim took his hand and squeezed. "I don't think you have anything to worry about, honey. You're an incredibly intelligent man and still as sharp as a tack. Like I said, stress may have played a part in this. Maybe you just had your mind on business and wasn't really 'there' with us that afternoon."

"That's not it!" he snapped, pulling his hand away. He instantly regretted being so anxious. "I'm sorry, Kim… but it's just not there." He flipped through the photos once more. They were like shots of his family acting out roles in a play that he knew absolutely nothing about. "I'm sacred. I don't know what to do." Absently, he rubbed at the back of his neck.

"Do you still have that stiffness? The soreness, too?"

Jay nodded. "Yep." He had suffered from a stiff neck and tenderness at the base of his skull since they moved into the house on Mesquite Lane a couple of weeks before. "Do you think that might be a symptom… of what's wrong with me?"

"Honestly, I don't know. If you're that concerned, go see a doctor," she urged. "Have a physical, or go to a neurological specialist if you want. Maybe this forgetfulness has a physical origin, and I don't mean Alzheimer's disease. You're a man of medicine, so you know it's better to be safe than sorry. Have these

things checked out before they progress into something more serious."

"I will," he promised, returning the strange photographs to their envelope. "I'll schedule an appointment tomorrow at the office."

"Good," she said, standing. "Now why don't you come and give me a hand in the kitchen? I'd like to get dinner done before Charlotte wakes up from her nap. It's impossible to chop onions and breastfeed at the same time, you know."

Jay nodded and, taking her hand again, accompanied her. "Okay, I can do that. The onion chopping… not the breast feeding."

A week following the incident with the photographs, Jay sat in the office of Tom Henderson, a leading neurologist in the Odessa area. He felt nervous, despite the fact that his physician's mind told him to approach his situation logically and without emotion. That was all well and fine when you were facing a patient. But when *you* were the patient, facing the prospect of a bad diagnosis, it was an entirely different ball game.

Fortunately, the smile on Henderson's face, as he walked in the door, told Jay that his anxiety was pointless.

"Well, all the tests came back negative, Jay," he told him. "You're fit as a fiddle."

"What about the memory loss?" Jay asked. "How do you explain that?"

"Have you had any incidents since the day you found the photos on the dining room table?"

"Yeah, a few," he admitted . "But nothing major. Just misplaced car keys and I've gone blank when dialing the phone lately, like I've lost track of who I was calling and what for."

"I do that myself from time to time," the doctor told him. "It's called middle-age. It's like a knife that dulls with use. Face it… after forty we're not as sharp as we used to be."

"So you don't think that I'm beginning to suffer the early stages of…"

"Alzheimer's?" Henderson shook his head. "I see no indication of that at all." He studied his paperwork and then looked up at his fellow physician. "You have a real fear of this, don't you?"

Jay felt foolish, but knew he must admit it. "Yes, I do."

"Maybe part of the problem is psychological," the specialist told him, flat out. "If you didn't seem to be such a stable and well-aligned person, I would recommend psychiatric help. But you do, so I won't."

"So, what do you suggest?"

"Don't push yourself so much," Henderson advised. "Take some time for yourself. Exercise more, get to bed early, and don't let the little things bug you so much."

Jay rubbed the nape of his neck. "And what about this pain I have? The stiffness?"

"Could be stress, plain and simple. But I'll take a look at it if you want."

Jay nodded and Henderson walked around to the rear of the examination table. He began to study the back of Jay's neck. After a long moment, the doctor said "Hmmm…"

"What's wrong?"

"Oh, nothing," Henderson told him. "But there is a spot where you've been rubbing. A swollen bump with a couple of tiny puncture wounds. A spider bite, more than likely."

"A *spider* bite? Are you certain?"

"Yeah, pretty sure. Do you have spiders at home? At your office?"

Jay thought for a moment. "Not at the office. The place is brand new... just opened four months ago. But, now that you mention it, I have seen a few spiders around the house. We bought a home in the Peyton Plains subdivision in Gardendale. It's not new... about thirty years old." He shuddered. "The spiders I've seen are sort of weird, not like your run-of-mill variety. They're white with a bright red streak down their back."

Henderson frowned. "Never heard of that kind before... not around these parts." He pulled a magnifier on an adjustable arm around and studied the bite closely. "Whatever it is, it looks harmless enough. There doesn't seem to be any tissue damage due to excessive poison... not like what a brown recluse would cause."

Jay couldn't help but shiver physically again. This time, his doctor noticed the reaction.

"Don't tell me that you have a fear of spiders, too."

"Yep," admitted Jay. "I'm deathly afraid of them. Have been ever since I was a kid."

"My suggestion is to hire a good exterminator and do away with these little white spiders," Henderson told him. "That will solve half of your problem, at least."

Jay hopped off the examination table. "Thanks, Tom. I appreciate it."

The neurologist shook his hand before he left. "If you have any more problems, just give me a call and we'll check them out."

Soon, Jay was leaving Dr. Henderson's office and heading down the hallway to the elevator. The tender spot on the back of his neck burned a little and he rubbed it.

An elderly Mexican man with a shock of thick silver hair and a bushy mustache was at the far end of the hall, waxing the floor with a rotary buffer. He paused for a moment and stared at him in an odd way... as though studying him.

Jay had seen the old man before. His name was Miguel and he did janitorial work for several of the medical centers and physician's offices in downtown Odessa. Puzzled by the man's interest, Jay stared back. Their eyes met uncomfortably for a second and a connection seemed to be made, although it was one that Jay couldn't seem to comprehend. He considered approaching the man and talking to him, but the worker dropped his gaze back to the floor and continued his waxing.

Jay shook his head, rubbed the back of his neck again, and entered the elevator for the trip to the parking garage below.

Several days passed without incident. Jay's worries slowly began to subside.

Then he awoke one night to find himself standing on the basement stairs, in pitch darkness.

He was so disoriented that he nearly fell down the wooden risers of the steps. At first he had no earthly idea where he was; the musky smell, the cool hardness of pine boards against the soles of his bare feet, an oppressive darkness crowding against his eyes. A moment of panic gripped him and he reached out for something to steady his balance. His hand found the wooden rail mounted diagonally along the right side of the wall. He gripped it tightly and, with the other hand, reached upward groping blindly, until he found the end of a dangling chain. He pulled it and, with a click, a sixty-watt bulb blazed overhead.

Yes, he *was* in the basement... or rather on the steep stairs leading down to the cellar. He and Kim had bought the house when he had taken the new position at the hospital. It was a two-story structure with an attached garage and an unfinished basement. They had been thinking about calling in a contractor and making the basement into a family room with a bedroom and bathroom for their teenage daughter. They knew Katie craved her privacy these days—what sixteen-year-old didn't?—and giving the girl her own little space might vanquish some of her drama queen tactics.

Still, the basement had always bothered Jay a little. He had only been down there twice. It was a long room, choked with the clutter of junk and cardboard boxes left behind by the former residents, surrounded by unfinished supports and cinderblock walls. Both times Jay had returned upstairs with a strange sensation, almost feeling as though he had invaded someone's territory and that someone had been watching him the whole time he had been down there. He knew that was silly and illogical, but he couldn't help but feel that way.

And he felt that way now, standing on the basement stairs in his pajamas.

What's wrong with me? he wondered as he realized exactly where he was. *What am I doing down here? Was I sleepwalking?* He gripped the handrail a little tighter, afraid that he might fall down the stairs.

The overhead bulb only illuminated the steps he was standing on. The light switch to the basement was at the base of the stairs. The cellar beyond was pitch black.

A noise echoed from below. Something moved in the darkness. A soft, dry *scuttling* sound.

Who is it? he considered asking out loud, but refrained from doing so. There was no one down there. No one at all. Maybe the sound had come from a mouse...or spiders.

A strange sense of disorientation gripped him at that moment. His mind grew cloudy and his vision blurred. Jay felt as though his skull was stuffed with cotton. *Am I having a stroke?* he wondered. But, no... he was a doctor and knew that none of the sensations he felt linked with the symptoms of a stroke. He felt something *pull* at his thoughts, almost like a fisherman's line tightening to reel in a stubborn catch, and, slowly, he took a couple of steps downward. *Where the hell am I going?* he asked himself. Soon, he would be at the bottom of the stairs in total darkness.

Below, he heard the scuttling sound increase in volume... moving over the cardboard boxes, across the concrete floor, along the bare wood of the rafters and the cinderblock walls.

The strange hold on his thoughts broke when he felt something crawl across the top of his left foot. He looked down to see one of those peculiar white spiders darting across his instep. Jay cried out and shook his foot violently until the spider lost its hold and was flung into the darkness of the basement.

Instantly, the scrabbling sound stopped. Only black silence occupied the depths of the cellar. But he sensed that it wouldn't last for long. Something told him that it would begin again, with renewed intensity and, perhaps, animosity.

Quickly, Jay turned and mounted the stairs. When he reached the top he pulled the chain, extinguishing the spare light of the overhead bulb. Then he ducked through the basement door and locked it securely behind him.

Jay returned to bed and nestled next to Kim, but was unable to drift back to sleep. He lay there, keenly aware of the darkness and the silence of the night around him. Something nagged at his thoughts again and he considered returning to the basement, although he couldn't understand his motivation for wanting to go there. He attempted to relax, but his nerves still tingled, tightly strung with the tension of his night-wandering.

He thought he heard a scuttling sound beneath the floor of the master bedroom, but couldn't say for sure.

The Memory Eater

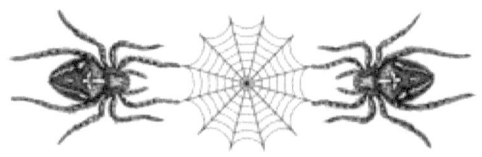

After that, things seemed to go steadily downhill for Jay Maher.

His concentration grew muddled and less focused, and his memory suffered sporadically. Needless to say, his declining mentality caused tension both at home and at work...not only for him, but everyone around him. He had gotten into and at work...not only for him, but everyone around him. He had gotten into several arguments with his wife and older daughter over misunderstandings caused by his flagging memory. And things were growing increasingly difficult at work, too.

It all seemed to come to a head one afternoon as he headed down a busy corridor for his office. He was navigating the traffic—doctors, nurses, patients, visitors—hoping to finish some paperwork before going home for the afternoon, when a woman's voice called out to him from behind.

"Dr. Maher? I can't believe it! What are you doing here?"

Jay turned around to find a young brunette in her late twenties, approaching him with a smile on her pretty face. A man of the same age, apparently her husband, followed her, equally pleased to see him.

"Pardon me?" asked Jay. He regarded the two strangers curiously, but also with a mounting sensation of dread.

"Here we flew to Odessa to be with my sister during her delivery and we find you here," the woman said. Without hesitation, she embraced him warmly. Jay stood there stiffly, unwilling to return the gesture. "It's been... how long?" she asked. "Four years? When the twins were born?"

The man reached out and shook Jay's hand firmly. "It's great seeing you again, Dr. Maher."

A cold feeling settled in the pit of the physician's stomach. *Good Lord, it's happening again!*

An awkward silence stretched between them; the couple smiling happily, while Jay frowned in utter bewilderment. Finally, he gathered up the nerve to say it. "Uh, do I know you two?"

Abruptly, the smiles on the couple's faces faded. Husband and wife looked at one another, and then back at the doctor again. "Dr. Maher... we're Sandra and Tom Brubaker. You saw us three times a week for four months." The brunette seemed upset. "You brought me through a difficult pregnancy with flying colors. You're the reason Brandon and Brian are alive today."

The blank expression on Jay's face brought an incredulous look from Tom Brubaker. "You.. you don't remember us, do you?"

Jay's heart pounded in his chest. "I'm sorry, but no, I don't."

Sandra was clearly hurt by his admission. "I can't believe that. You took such good care of me those four months. You even came to the hospital at three in the morning when I went into labor, just to see me through the delivery. You... you were kind of like a father to me."

Jay opened his mouth, but said nothing. He simply shrugged his shoulders.

Tom's eyes were angry as he put his arm around his wife's trembling shoulders. "We thought you were different, Dr. Maher. You seemed genuinely concerned about us and the babies. But I reckon you're just like a lot of other doctors these days... putting on an act just for the sake of a paycheck."

Jay searched his memory for some shred of the past that would connect to the young couple who stood before him. But, no matter how hard he tried, it simply wouldn't come. "I'm terribly sorry, but I just don't remember."

Angry and hurt, the two turned and left him standing in the middle of the corridor. Jay felt a wave of panic rush over him. He saw the door of the men's room a few yards away and was soon out of the busy hallway and leaning against a sink opposite a row of toilet stalls. He stared at his face in the mirror and saw a pale, frightened version of the confident physician he once was. He turned on the tap and splashed water on his face, washing away the cold sweat that had collected on his brow.

What's happening to me? Am I going insane?

Then, suddenly, in the reflection of the mirror, he noticed that he was not alone in the restroom. He was surprised to find that it was the elderly custodian, Miguel, who stood within the open door of a toilet stall staring at him, a cleaning rag in one brown hand and a spray bottle of cleaning disinfectant in the other.

Miguel stooped and set his supplies on the tile floor, then walked toward the doctor. Jay could do nothing but stand there, his back to the man, as he advanced. The old Mexican had a grim expression on his mustachioed face as he came within reach and lifted his hand. It was at that moment that Jay realized that the man was not looking at him as a whole, but at a single focal point.

He was studying the back of his neck.

"No... don't," Jay said, but his protest came as a low, weak whisper.

Miguel ignored his words. Soon, the man's calloused fingertips touched the point of interest; the tender spot at the base of Jay's skull. A spot that had gradually grown into a small, hard knot during the past two weeks.

"Spider bite?" the man asked softly.

Jay swallowed dryly. "Yes... how did you know?"

The old man turned Jay around by his shoulders until the two stood face to face. Then he took the doctor's right hand and lifted it, over his shoulder, to the back of his own neck. There, in the exact same spot as Jay's knot, was one of his own. It felt as though it had been there for a long time, thick and roughly the size and hardness of a golf ball.

"How?" Jay muttered. "When?"

Miguel looked around and, certain that no one else was in the bathroom with them, began to speak. "Forty years ago, across the border. Some friends and I were coming to Texas to work and we camped in the desert, near an abandoned shack by some railroad tracks. The following morning, we awoke and found ourselves starting life anew... with no recollection of our former lives. If we had wives and children back in Mexico, those memories were erased. We knew our names and that was all." He reached around and rubbed the fleshy knot on the back of his neck. "But we all shared one thing in common. We had all been bitten by something in the dead of night. Something horrible."

"What was it? Did you know?"

Miguel shook his head. "No, not at first. It wasn't until a few days later that we happened upon a fellow countryman... one ancient in years and wise. He sensed our dilemma and told us the nature of our lost lives." The old man's hand trembled as it drew away from the protruding spot on the back of his neck. "He told us that it was an evil that has roamed this earth for many centuries . An evil that makes the Serpent in Eden's garden seem like a playful earthworm in comparison. A creature called *Vuelvase Memoria*."

Jay knew enough Spanish to translate the phrase without difficulty. "The Memory Eater."

"Yes," Miguel rasped softly, his eyes brimming with bitterness. "A monster that covets the hopes and dreams of men and draws sustenance from siphoning their memories from the inner recesses of their minds."

"But, you said spider bite..."

"That is right. The Vuelvase Memoria's minions—his instruments for extracting memories—are like spiders in appearance."

"*White* spiders," gasped Jay.

Miguel nodded solemnly. "Yes. Tiny white spiders about as big as a man's thumbnail. Sometimes the Memory Eater uses them discreetly, taking a man's memory little by little, one night at a time." The elderly man shuddered. "But sometimes it will come under its own power and hunger, and attack a man during the course of a single twilight. Then it takes all that it can get and departs, leaving its victim full of fear and vacant thoughts. Just as it did that night four decades ago, to me and seven of my fellow amigos."

Jay shook his head, his logical self rebelling against what the old man had just told him. "I'm not sure that I can believe in this Vuelvase Memoria, even after what has happened to me."

"Do you believe that God exists?" Miguel asked him. "And the Devil?"

The doctor was not a religious man, but he did hold basic theological beliefs. "Yes, I do."

"Then you must believe in this entity as well, for it is a small and terrible god itself."

"And you believe this thing came out of the desert? Or from that shack beside the railroad tracks?"

"According to the man who told us of Vuelvase Memoria, the fiend dwells in places devoid of light… in abandoned structures or locations where humans rarely go." He studied Jay's face. "Tell me, doctor… do you have such a place where you live? An old outbuilding on your property that is no longer in use?"

Suddenly, Jay thought of the incident of several nights ago; of awakening, startled, on the cellar stairs. "No, but I do have an unfinished basement where no one goes."

"Then that is the lair of the Memory Eater and his army of thieves. Listen to me carefully. You must tell me everything that has happened. The safety and sanity of you and your entire family could depend on what you tell me here and now."

Jay took a deep breath and, over the next ten minutes, told the old man his story. When he was finished, he felt drained.

Miguel nodded silently, digesting the information that he had been privy to. "Then I shall help you... before it is too late and you end up as I have; a lonely shell of a man who no longer knows where he came from or those who love him in that unknown place."

"You can destroy this thing?" Jay asked him.

"No, but I can drive it away," Miguel replied. "Out of your house and your life. The man who told us of Vuelvase Memoria took me under his wing. He taught me of its strengths and weaknesses... of things that it both craves and loathes."

"And the memories it has taken? Will I get them back?"

Doubt showed in the old man's eyes. "I cannot guarantee that, señor, but it is possible. If we can distress it enough, it may very well release what is yours before it makes its escape." Miguel's face was clearly frightened. "That is, if all goes well. If it doesn't, both of us could possibly lose all that we now possess and be as a slate wiped completely clean."

"When can you come?" Jay asked him. "I don't know if I could spend another night in that house... knowing what is down in that basement."

"I will come tonight," Miguel promised. "I must make preparations first, but I should be there by seven o'clock at the very latest."

Jay gave Miguel his address and the two exchanged cell phone numbers. As an afterthought, the doctor reached out and shook his hand. "Thank for helping me with this."

The elderly man smiled humorlessly, displaying crooked, yellow teeth. "I must admit, señor, my motives for doing so are not completely benevolent. I have my own hopes and dreams to consider."

Then Jay departed the restroom, leaving the custodian to continue with his work.

The Memory Eater

Jay normally worked until five or five-thirty in the evening, but his conversation with Old Miguel and his concern for the well-being of his family, caused him to head home early that afternoon. He arrived home around 2:45.

He walked through the front door to the sound of a baby screaming in the nursery at the rear of the house.

His heart pounding, Jay left the foyer and mounted the stairs to the upper floor, taking two risers at a time. "Kim!" he called out. "Kim, where are you?"

His wife replied from the room at the far end of the upstairs hallway. "In here, Jay." Her voice sounded small and frightened, strung taut with anxiety and confusion.

When he reached the nursery, he burst through the door. The room looked as it had that morning when he had sneaked in and gave the baby a good-bye kiss. Pink and frilly with a princess motif; pumpkin-shaped carriages, lofty castles, and cartoonish woodland animals. His wife was sitting in the glider-rocker in the far corner, her face bathed with tears and her hands fidgeting in her lap.

"What's wrong with Charlotte?" he asked her.

Kim shook her head. "I don't know. She woke up from her nap screaming like a banshee. And every time I come near the crib, she gets even more upset. You're the doctor, Jay. Tell me what's wrong with her!"

Jay walked to the crib and peered down at the squirming form of his eight-month-old daughter. Her face was beet red as she shrieked without ceasing. "What's the matter, little angel?" he asked, reaching down for her.

As his hands drew nearer, her eyes widened in terror and her crying increased in volume and fury.

"What is it?" Kim demanded. She stood up, but kept her distance, as though afraid to venture any nearer. "What's wrong with our baby?"

Jay studied the infant for a long moment. Then he grew cold inside. "She's afraid of us."

"What do you mean 'afraid of us'? That's crazy! Why would she be afraid of her mother and father?"

"Because she doesn't *remember* us," he told her. He motioned his wife to join him. At first, Kim was hesitant. But, eventually, she made her way to her daughter's bedside. "Here… turn her over on her stomach. I want to examine the back of her neck."

Kim stared at him. "Back of her neck? Why do you…?"

"Please… just do as I ask."

His wife complied and, with some effort, wrestled Charlotte onto her belly. They didn't have to do much searching to find what they were looking for. A swollen pink lump showed just beneath her hairline, at the base of her skull.

"Oh, God, Jay… what is that?" Kim asked, her voice scarcely a whisper.

A spider bite, he almost said, but refrained from doing so. He didn't want to upset Kim any more than she already was. "You stay here with Charlotte," he told her. "I need to make a call."

His wife looked frightened and uncertain. She released her infant daughter and stepped back. The baby girl flipped onto her back, kicking and screaming. "Okay," she said, "I'll just sit over here." Kim backtracked to the rocker and curled up against its cushions.

Jay left the nursery and headed for the staircase. He was almost there when his oldest daughter appeared at the head of the stairs, her school backpack slung over her shoulder.

"What's the matter with Charlotte?" Katie asked him. "I could hear her screaming her lungs out from outside the house."

"Go to the nursery and help Mom with the baby, will you?" her father requested. "Shut the door and don't open it until I get back."

"But what's going on?"

"Please, sweetheart... just do as I ask. Okay?"

Katie nodded, looking more than a little spooked. "Sure, Dad."

As the teenager made her way down the upstairs hallway, Jay made his way downstairs. When he reached the foyer, he took his cell phone from his pocket and dialed a number while he paced back and forth.

A moment later, someone answered. "Hello?"

Jay could hardly talk at first. His throat felt bone dry. He took a couple of swallows and cleared his throat. "Miguel? This is Dr. Maher. One of the spiders has bitten my baby daughter. She's scared to death of us, because she doesn't know who we are."

There was a stretch of silence on the line. Then Miguel spoke. "I have nearly gathered all that we will need. Give me another half hour, señor Maher, and I will be there. And we will drive away this evil creature and its awful thievery of the mind."

"I hope so," said Jay. "I'll be waiting."

"Half an hour and I will be there."

After the call, the doctor sat down heavily on the lower steps of the staircase to wait. Thirty minutes wasn't a lengthy period of time, but given the circumstances, it seemed like an eternity to Jay Maher.

The rapping of knuckles on the front door caused Jay to leap from his place on the staircase. A second later, he was wrenching the door open. Old Miguel stood there, still dressed in his gray work clothes, a grim expression on his wrinkled face. He held a leather bag in his right hand. It was stained and weathered, clearly ancient in both appearance and origin.

"Are you prepared to lay eyes on something your mind may not wish to accept?" the Mexican asked him. "And to drive it from the sanctity of your home?"

"Yes, I am."

Miguel nodded solemnly. As Jay led him down the passageway beside the staircase toward the rear of the house, he could hear the elderly man mumbling to himself. At first, Jay was sure that it was merely gibberish, but then he recognized it for what it truly was; a prayer of some kind, but in some language other than Spanish.

When they reached the cellar door, Miguel nodded toward the door at the rear of the utility room, which led to the back deck and the grassy lawn just beyond. "Prop that door open," he instructed. "So that the bastardo has a clear route to make its departure."

Jay did as he requested. He opened the back door and propped it open with a case of bottled water that sat against the wall next to the washer and dryer. When he turned he found that Miguel had opened the basement door. He stood there on the threshold, staring into the darkness below.

"Do you have a flashlight, señor Maher?" he asked, not bothering to look his way. His right hand dipped into the leather bag and retrieved a pint canning jar of a reddish powder.

"Yes, but there is a light at the top of the stairway," Jay told him.

"I already tried it. The bulb has been shattered." Miguel grinned humorlessly. "They know that we are coming for them."

Jay opened a cabinet over the washing machine and found a Maglite lying between a jug of Tide and a box of fabric softener sheets. He depressed the switch to make sure the batteries were still strong. They were. The light blazed brightly from the glass lens of its head.

"Okay... I've got it."

"Then let's go," Miguel said. He unscrewed the top of the jar and poured a bit of the reddish powder into the palm of hand. "Shine the light over my shoulder, so I can see where I'm going. But keep close… don't stray too far behind. And leave the cellar door open."

Jay nodded and followed the old man's instructions to the letter. He thought of Kim, Katie, and Charlotte in the nursery upstairs and prayed that they did as they had been told and stayed put. If they decided to come downstairs for some reason… well, he simply didn't want to think of what might take place.

Miguel flung a fistful of the red powder down the risers of the steps and then started downward. "Remember, close and silent. Say nothing."

"Yes," said Jay, his voice scarcely a whisper.

The two began to descend the basement stairs. With each step downward, Jay felt that, in some horrible way, they were approaching the very gates of Hell itself.

When they made the cellar, Jay reached past Miguel and tried the light switch there. Again, only an impotent click and darkness. Jay swung the beam of the flashlight in a wide arch. Everything seemed to be as it was the last time he had been there; the box-cluttered floor with only a narrow aisle of concrete showing, the naked rafters of the ceiling overhead, the barren block walls stretching on all sides.

I don't see anything, he wanted to say, but didn't. He adhered to his promise of silence and followed Miguel, holding the Maglite high to illuminate the way. His ears were keen, listening for the tiniest sound. He heard it a second later; the scuttling sound of multi-legged things moving en masse at the far side of the lower level.

Jay was shifting the beam toward a shadowy entrance in the far end of the basement—an empty chamber of cinderblock foundation beneath the house's front porch—when the Mexican laid his hand across the flashlight and pushed its light toward the floor. Jay's breath instantly froze in his chest, unable to escape for a tense moment.

A tide of tiny white spiders was racing toward them… filling the narrow aisle, surging over boxes and crates, their albino bodies gleaming in the battery-powered glow of the hand-held light.

Jay considered the option of running back up the stairs, gathering his family, and leaving the house, never to return. But two things stopped him. His faith in the old man that he accompanied and his desire to have his lost memories returned to him… as well as those of his newborn daughter.

Miguel poured a generous amount of the red dust into his palm and scattered it across the floor and the sides of the boxes, a few feet in front of the advancing swarm. He motioned for Jay to step back, then did so himself. The two men watched as the spiders made contact with the mysterious crimson powder. One by one, the spiders vanished in a bright pinpoint of light. And, with each demise, a sharp pain ripped through Jay's mind, as though someone was jabbing needles into the flesh of his brain.

He glanced over and saw, from the agonized expression on Miguel's ancient face, that he was experiencing the same thing. Before long, the arachnid army of Vuelvase Memoria was no more, gone in a pall of blue flash and sulfur.

"The hateful thing is there," Miguel said softly. He pointed the narrow entrance and the dark shadows within its hollow. The old man rummaged through his leather pouch and produced two objects. One was a small, black book that, at first, resembled a Bible. But, upon further inspection, Jay could tell that it was a tome that was not nearly as comforting or benevolent as God's Word. The book's covers were thick and deeply embossed with symbols unlike any he had ever seen before, and the wrinkled pages were held tightly in place with ornate hinges that looked to be constructed of tarnished gold.

The second object was another glass jar, this one larger than the one that had held the red powder. Inside where bluish-purple spheres the size of sparrow eggs. Miguel tucked the book beneath

his arm and unscrewed the top of the jar. A hiss of pent-up air was released as the seal was broken and a terrible stench drifted from the open mouth of the container. It smelled like a mixture of fresh feces and roadkill that had baked for a day in a hot August sun.

Miguel handed Jay the jar and kept the book for himself. "What are these things?" the doctor couldn't help but wonder out loud.

"Ammunition," Miguel said softly. "Not to kill, but to wound. To drive out the monster that has taken refuge here."

Jay tucked the flashlight in the cradle of his right armpit and, holding the jar in both hands, followed Miguel across the cluttered floor of the basement. The elderly man unclasped the book and opened it to a center page. He began to read in a loud, clear voice. The words that rolled off his tongue were alien to Jay, almost holding a chanting, sing-song quality to them. It was unlike any language the doctor had ever heard before.

Miguel looked over and saw the question in Jay's eyes. "Ancient Mayan," he explained. "The civilization that first spawned the horror of Vuelvase Memoria."

The nearer they got to their destination, the harder it seemed to be able to walk. Jay felt a dark blanket threaten to engulf his mind. His thoughts grew disjointed and his movements became sluggish, as though he was traveling through a muddy bog than across the flat hard surface of a concrete floor.

"It seeks to stop us," rasped Miguel, shaking his head to clear his own thoughts. "Breathe deeply and clear your mind. If it paralyzes us into submission, it will do with us as it pleases."

The thought horrified Jay, both for his sake and that of his family. He fought against the exhaustion and confusion that threatened to engulf his mind and body, and trudged onward.

Finally, they reached the dark doorway that led to the recess beneath the porch. Inside they heard something move... something very large. "When we step through the doorway, I will read the incantation and you will throw the objects at Vuelvase Memoria.

Throw them as hard and fast as you can, just as you would a baseball. They must penetrate its essence to be effective."

Jay's hand trembled as he dipped his fingers through the mouth of the jar and grasped one of the malodorous spheres. It felt soft and waxy between his fingertips and, for an instant, it seemed as though something just beneath its leathery surface *pulsated.* Jay didn't dwell on what might be nestled within each bluish-purple sphere. He didn't want to know.

"Now!" ordered Miguel. Together, they entered the narrow entrance. They found themselves standing in a cramped chamber of dank concrete roughly twelve feet by eight feet. The beam of Jay's flashlight swung wildly, jittering, as it eventually settled on the hideous form of Vuelvase Memoria… the dreaded Memory Eater.

The thing was vile in appearance and humongous in size. In some ways it resembled a spider, with bulbous hindquarters and eight long, spindly legs. But other aspects of the creature reminded Jay of some massive amoeba; pale and translucent, with a soft jelly-like consistency to its flesh… if you could even classify it as such. What terrified the doctor the most was the fiend's massive head. A multitude of glassy eyes of all sizes and hues engulfed the upper half of its skull, while sharp, spiky mandibles occupied the lower half. They gnashed against one another, sounding like a knife grating against a whetstone.

"Now!" yelled Miguel, also clearly horrified by the creature clinging to the concrete walls before them. "Throw!"

Jay cocked his arm to throw and, in the process, dropped the flashlight that had been tucked beneath his right armpit. The Maglite hit the concrete floor, then bounced and rolled across the floor. In the gloom, the pale mass of Vuelvase Memoria detached itself from the wall and shambled toward them.

Although the skewed beam of the lost flashlight denied Miguel enough light to read from the book, he continued anyway, reciting the incantation by memory. In turn, Jay lobbed the first sphere at the body of the creature. It hit the thing's gelatinous flesh and, at first, simply lodged there. Then, slowly the object sank into the depths of the Memory Eater's rancid body, disappearing from sight. Almost instantly, a violent bluish-white flash shown from somewhere inside it. The sphere had ruptured and done its damage. The creature shrieked, but not outwardly. Its shrill cries of agony ripped through Jay's mind, rather than his ears.

"Again, señor Maher!" commanded Miguel. "Again!"

One after another, Jay dug the oily spheres from the Mason jar and threw them directly at the approaching beast. The objects penetrated the monster's translucent flesh and immediately burst in flashpoints of blue-white brilliance. The thing's wails of agony and defeat filled Jay's thoughts, threatening to crumble the very foundation of his sanity.

Then Miguel motioned for him to retreat to the far end of the porch's sub-chamber. "Give it room to pass by. It is making its escape."

As the two men plastered themselves against the concrete wall, they watched as the thing reached the narrow opening that led into the basement and squeezed through. They stood in the shadows, afraid to move, listening to the sound of boxes and crates overturning in its wake. When they finally gathered the nerve to go to the doorway and look out, they found that the thing was dragging itself up the stairs, one riser at a time. It wasn't long before it was completely out of sight.

By the time Jay and Miguel crossed the basement floor and reached the top of the stairs, the creature had escaped across the utility room floor, leaving a slimy, grayish residue upon the stone tile, and out the back door of the house. They emerged onto the rear deck to hear the barking of neighborhood dogs, disturbed at the stench of a living thing they had never caught wind of before… and probably never would again in their lifetimes.

They caught a quick glimpse of the thing scuttling over the backyard privacy fence... and then it was gone.

Suddenly, Jay felt a peculiar sensation in his head; a sensation not unlike the change of pressure in your ears when rising to a higher elevation. A flood of lost memories coursed through his mind... memories that simply hadn't been there before. Feeling disoriented, Jay grabbed hold of the deck railing to steady himself. "It's all coming back to me!" he said in amazement. "I remember now."

When Miguel failed to answer, Jay turned and regarded the old man. Tears trickled down the cheeks of his weathered face.

"So do I," he said softly, his lips trembling.

A few days later, Jay Maher found himself at Midland International Airport, seeing off a friend. A friend who had been a stranger a short time before, but was now as cherished as a member of his own family.

Miguel looked down at the plane ticket in his hand. "I am very grateful for this, señor Maher."

"Jay," the doctor corrected.

"... Jay. But you shouldn't have."

"It's little to give, considering all that you gave back to me and my family. Thank you."

Jay could tell that the old man was both excited and apprehensive about returning home. According to Miguel, he had a family back in Juarez; a family he had lost for forty years, but had now rediscovered. A wife, three grown children, and a dozen grandchildren. Of course, it would be difficult and awkward to return to such a life after so long an absence, but at least now he knew who he had been back in Mexico and what he had left behind.

"Well, you'd better get to the security check," Jay said. "You know how long that takes these days."

Miguel nodded. His eyes gleamed beneath busy gray brows. "I am glad I was cleaning toilets in the men's room that day."

"So am I. You can't imagine how glad." The two hesitated for a moment and then embraced warmly.

When they separated, Jay checked his watch. "Well, I've got to get out of here."

"Something special planned?" Miguel asked.

"Yes. I'm going on a picnic," Jay Maher said with a smile. "And this time I'm going to enjoy—and remember—every moment of it."

Housewarming

Exactly why Aunt Millie had willed him the house on Elkins Avenue was something Chuck Stuart had been trying to figure out since the old woman's funeral. He had finally concluded that she had done so purely out of spite.

Chuck had never been one of his late aunt's favorite nephews. As a teenager, his constant rebellion against authority had always rubbed her strict religious values the wrong way. Quite a few unsavory episodes in his wild lifestyle had distanced him and his aunt during the years and perhaps that was the main reason she had stuck him with that unsalable property on the low-rent side of town.

Yes, the single-story house on the half acre lot was completely without market value and for one distinct reason. It was infested with spiders. Brown recluse spiders they were, sometimes called fiddlebacks because of the pale violin shape across their back. They were poisonous little devils; not as much so as a black widow, but close. They had a nasty bite to them, causing nerve and tissue damage and, if there was an allergic reaction, death.

Aunt Millie had lived there until five years ago, when Uncle Pete died. Then she had moved into an apartment and rented the little white clapboard house to various low-income families from time to time. Her property in west Nashville had netted her six

Housewarming

hundred bucks monthly... until the spider problem began. It had gotten so bad, in fact, that the tenants had finally gotten fed up and moved out, leaving their possessions behind.

Several exterminators had been hired to fumigate the entire house, but it didn't seem to do any good. In a month's time their number had increased tenfold. It got to the point where his aunt was scared to even venture into the house herself. She could see the spiders clustered on the inside of the windows, skittering across the whitewashed siding outside and up the rain gutters. Finally, she had closed up the house permanently, stapling sheets of clear plastic over the doors and windows until it looked as though it was encased in cellophane, hermetically sealed against the outer world. Millie would have had the place torn down, but no demolition crew would go near it. Many a dozer operator got cold feet thinking about plowing into that old house and becoming immediately covered with the tiny brown spiders.

And now Chuck was checking the place out for himself. The only reason he was there was because of his own desperation. Chuck's financial situation was pretty depressing. He was a session musician by trade and a good one. He worked the recording studios along Music Row, playing lead guitar and fiddle whenever the demand arose. Lately it had not, and he found himself living uncomfortably beyond his means.

Therefore, he figured he might weasel out of the lease on his own riverfront apartment and live there for a while. That was if those hair-raising tales about spider infestation panned out as being just another one of his late aunt's vivid exaggerations. She had been quite infamous for making mountains out of molehills.

Chuck eyed the house with apprehension as he walked up the weedy sidewalk and climbed the porch. The front door was blocked by a wrinkled sheet of heavy plastic, the type painters used for drop cloths. Chuck unfolded his pocketknife and split it down the center, watching nervously for the first sign of spiders. So far nothing. He dug the keys from his pocket, unlocked the door and, armed with a flashlight and a can of heavy-duty spider spray, stepped into the cramped and stuffy living room.

The room was dark and dusty, the blinds drawn and the second-hand furniture sitting in shadowy lumps, deserted by the previous tenants. There was even a color television in the far corner. *Cripes, they must have been in a hell of a big hurry to get out of here*, he concluded. He directed his light upon the dusty floorboards, along the drapes and the uneven plaster walls. But still there was no visible sign of those nasty fiddlebacks.

He took the grand tour of the place, vaguely remembering it from the times he had visited there as a child. It was a small house built in the post-war forties. Just a living room, a couple of bedrooms, a bathroom, and a kitchen. As he entered each room, he expected to see fleeting movement and the corners shrouded in tattered web. But, except for the light powdering of dust and the rancid smell of mildew, the house seemed perfectly normal.

Chuck breathed a sigh of relief and smirked at his aunt's stupidity. *The joke's on you, dear aunt*, he thought with a shake of his head. *There aren't any spiders here. Hell, I haven't seen a single spider since I walked into this damned place.*

On the spur of the moment he decided to rush home, pack a few things, and spend the night there. Sort of a trial run and a further snubbing of his late relative's groundless phobia of spiders. There would be no electricity, but he could rough it for a couple of nights at least.

He examined the master bedroom. There he found a sturdy wood-framed bed, complete with mattress. He sat down and bounced a few times, testing the springs. *It'll do till I can tote my bed over. Yeah, this might not turn out so shabby after all.*

Housewarming

The next few days passed without incident. It was the nocturnal hours spent in the old house, however, that kept Chuck from the creature comfort of a single good night's sleep.

He would awaken in the early hours of the morning, peering alertly into pitch darkness, his ears straining for the least little sound. He often thought he could hear the minute scrambling of thousands of tiny legs as they skittered somewhere beneath him. He could almost sense the movement en masse. But when he took his flashlight from the nightstand and shone it upon the floor beneath his bed, there would be nothing but shadow and dust bunnies. No milling multitude of venomous arachnids… only emptiness.

The following morning found him, with flashlight and insecticide, thoroughly searching the entire house, from attic to the cramped crawlspace of the foundation. As always, he found nothing. Rather than dispelling his suspicions, his fruitless inspections only caused the feeling of unease to grow even stronger.

He could not understand it. All the neighbors he had talked to had confirmed Aunt Millie's story. According to them, the little house had been hopelessly invaded by brown recluse spiders. Yet, he had found no evidence of there ever having been a single one in the vicinity. None of the tell-tale signs were revealed; tatters of old webbing, dried bugs who had fallen prey, not even a single, shriveled husk of a long-dead fiddleback.

Still, Chuck could not shake that unnerving sensation that they were there somewhere, luring just beyond the reach of prying eyes.

Such a vast nest of the horrid pests could not have disappeared so completely and left no lingering trace at all.

The utilities were back on by Friday and, on Saturday morning, Chuck recruited some friends to help him move. A U-Haul and two trips transferred all his earthly belongings from the excessively expensive apartment to the drafty bungalow halfway across town.

They had most of the stuff unpacked and put away by nightfall and, during the hectic process, Chuck had mentioned several times for everyone to "watch out for spiders". It soon became an inside joke with the gang. One of the girls would let out a squeal and Chuck would come running with a fly-swatter and a can of spider spray. Everyone would break up laughing. Chuck didn't think it was so damned funny at first, but soon he joined in, feeling foolish and a little peeved at himself for being so nervous over a creature no larger than his thumb.

That night they had a party to celebrate Chuck's new residence. He pulled out all the stops and told his friends to cut loose and enjoy themselves. There was some coke and grass, plenty of booze, and, after hooking up the stereo system, they cranked up the volume and jammed to everything from Led Zeppelin to Lynyrd Skynyrd. Chuck's blatant disregard for restraint was not so much directed at his new neighbors than it was directed at Aunt Millie herself. The rock & roll orgy was his final rebellion; thumbing his nose at her stifling, puritanical ways and her last-ditch effort to put him down with that silly story of wholesale spider infestation.

Chuck was half bombed and just starting to loosen up, when his girlfriend, Bonnie, let out a shriek and bounded off the couch, rubbing the back of her arm.

"What's the matter, sweetheart?" he asked in sudden, sober concern.

"I don't know," she pouted. "Felt like something bit me."

"Better break out the Raid, Chuck!" some joker yelled and started an uproar. Only Chuck and Bonnie didn't laugh. He examined the welt on her arm and found it red and inflamed. Almost instantly he knew exactly what had bitten her.

"Grab your jacket," he told her. "I'm taking you to the emergency room. You've got a bad spider bite there."

That brought a few giggles from the half-stoned crowd. "Oooh, there he goes with those freaking spiders again!" snorted his best friend, Ted Downes, who was taking a Metallica CD from its case.

Chuck's face grew livid with sudden rage. "Just shut the hell up, will you?" His words sent the whole group into stunned silence. "Listen up! This party is officially over. I'm taking Bonnie to the hospital and when I get back I want to see this place vacant... understand?"

Everyone nodded and mumbled their agreement. "What about your bed?" asked Ted. "I thought we were gonna set it up for you tonight?"

"I'll get it myself tomorrow." Chuck had calmed down a little and felt like a complete ass for flying off the handle. "Really, I appreciate everyone's help today. It's just been a very tiring day for me with the move and all."

"Sure, man, we understand," assured Ted. "You go on and take your lady to the doctor. We'll stick around long enough to clean up and we'll lock the door when we leave."

Chuck offered an appreciative smile. "Thanks. We'll see you guys later."

Everyone sat in silence until they heard Chuck's Corvette pull out of the drive. "Now let's do some serious partying!" shouted Ted. He pushed the volume control to the limit and, with a girl on each arm, proceeded to open a fresh keg.

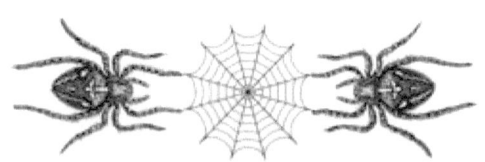

Chuck was in a foul mood when he returned home later that night. It was not because he found the place in worse shape than when he had left. He had expected as much from reliable ol' Ted. No, it was the hassle he had gone through at the hospital that lay heavily on his thoughts.

He had a hard time convincing the attending physician in the ER that Bonnie had been bitten by a brown recluse. "Are you absolutely sure?" the young doctor had asked. "Did you kill the spider? Did you even see it?" Chuck had answered no and, when the doctor first refused to treat the wound as a spider bite, he had nearly decked the guy, he was so keyed up.

Finally, Bonnie's injury had been treated as such and Chuck had driven her home. She had wanted to stay the night at his place, despite the possibility of another spider bite. After some heated discussion, Chuck had given in. He told her to come over around midnight. That would give him plenty of time to check out the house before she showed up, although he had a sinking feeling that he knew what he would find, or rather, not find when his search was complete.

The first thing he did when he got there was tear the cushions from the sofa and pull it away from the wall. He examined it thoroughly but found nothing. In frustration and total disgust, he retired to the bedroom.

He lay in bed and watched television, waiting until the hour of twelve rolled around. The nightly news first, then an old Gunsmoke rerun. He was drifting off, when something caught his attention and made his heart pound in excitement. A tiny, star-shaped shadow darted across the TV screen, settled on Matt Dillon's face for a second, then disappeared into the dark border of the picture tube.

Chuck was up in a flash, the lights on, a rolled-up TV Guide clutched in one hand. He crossed the floor to the set and searched

Housewarming

it, front and back. He found no sign of the fleeting intruder. "Where are you, you little bastard?" he grumbled.

He pulled the TV stand away from the wall. There was a small crack in the baseboard, just large enough for a spider to squeeze through. His awful obsession came to a head at that moment, turning him a little crazy. He stepped into the hallway and found the toolbox he had brought to do some carpentry work. He took a claw hammer back into the bedroom with him and set to work.

After ten minutes, he finally ran out of steam and stared dumbly at his destructive handiwork. He had torn away the oaken baseboard along the bottom and battered several large craters in the plastered drywall. His violent mutilation had revealed only aged insulation and a few random mouse turds abandoned along the studs and crossbeams. And guess what? That's right. Not one freaking spider!

Chuck stumbled into the bathroom and downed a couple of Tylenols for his blinding headache. "Chill out, man," he told himself. "You're getting all worked up over nothing." He glared into the mirror and saw the face of a haunted man. *I bet Aunt Millie is really getting a kick out of this. I bet she's laughing her ass off up there in the great hereafter. Well, screw you, dear auntie! This is my place now; lock, stock, and barrel. Your little head game with the spider story isn't going to work anymore. I'm here to stay, you old bitch, and there's nothing you can do about it!*

Wearily, he prepared for bed. He stripped down and, naked, climbed into bed and switched off the nightstand lamp. He did not feel like waiting up for Bonnie any longer. She would likely wake him up at midnight anyway, with that wicked little way of hers. Not that he would feel much like accommodating her affections tonight. The day's activities had pretty much wasted him.

He sighed deeply and settled between the cool sheets, hoping that sleep would come soon. He had left the side window open. It was cool that night, but comfortably so. The sound of crickets and a southbound train lulled him into a light slumber.

Chuck was awakened abruptly an hour later when a spring poked him square in the lower back. "Damned mattress!" he rasped. He managed to find a more comfortable position, but not for long. Two more springs jutted upward, prodding him the left shoulder blade and right buttock. "What the hell is going on here?" he asked the darkness, then suddenly held his breath.

He could feel the mattress moving slightly beneath his weight, could sense something vibrant and alive stirring against his body, separated only by thin foam padding and cloth. Goosebumps prickled his naked flesh and he nearly cried out as the loud ripping of rotten mattress ticking echoed from beneath the bedcovers.

Almost afraid to move, Chuck reached for the flashlight that sat on the nightstand. He snapped on the light, lifted the covers, and, in horror, shone its beam at the foot of the bed.

A great gorge of writhing, brown spiders spewed from the split in the old mattress. He wanted to scream, wanted to leap from the cool bed linen, but dared not. He dared not whimper a sound or move a muscle. He dropped the flashlight and endured the awful sensation of those tiny abominations as they danced across his ankles.

Like an incoming tide, the spiders advanced upon him in brown ripples, covering his legs, groin, the flat of his stomach. He could only lie there and shudder as they covered him completely, taking up every available inch of bare flesh, each one claiming its own private spot.

When the maddening tickle of tiny legs ceased to cross his skin, Chuck laid there in rigid suspense. *What the hell are they doing?* screamed his mind. *In God's name, what are they waiting for?*

A signal. That was what they were waiting for. When the last fiddleback had taken its proper place, the link was complete. As if on cue from some higher state of consciousness, they all began to bite, pumping every pore with the vile poison of their glands. Chuck's body lurched violently, racked in agony, his nervous system pierced by a thousand white-hot needles. But it was only for a second. The deadening effect of the venom acted fast, plunging him into merciful paralysis.

Then they were on the move once again. Scampering through his hair, invading every orifice of his body; his ears, his nasal passages, the gaping cave of his mouth, frozen in a final silent scream. They squeezed past the loosening muscles of his rectum and made a mad dash through the twisting maze of his bowels. A platoon of baby spiders entered the opening at the tip of his penis and traveled through the channel of the shaft, marching their way toward the warm nursery of his bladder.

Slowly, one by one, they began to settle into their newfound home.

The fleeting wash of headlights passed the bedroom window as a car pulled into the driveway outside. The sudden glow revealed a picture hanging on the far wall… a picture that Chuck swore had not been hanging there before. It was the smug and self-righteous face of Aunt Millie. A faded black-and-white photograph wreathed in a squirming frame of brown recluse spiders.

Abruptly, fiddlebacks settled on his unflinching eyeballs and he laid there in total darkness. He listened torturously for the sound of Bonnie's key in the front door lock, the sound of her footsteps in the hallway, the rustle of her clothing as she disrobed and climbed into bed next to him.

And he knew there would be nothing he could possibly do to warn her.

Atomic Arachnid Armageddon!

Jerry Perrigo's dad drove them to the Limelight Theater in his '57 Chevy Bel-Air. The windows were rolled all the way down and the warm June air ruffled their hair and made them squint. Normally, the Perrigos' golden retriever, Trevor, rode in the passenger seat alongside the driver, his head hanging out the window and his tongue flapping in the breeze. But not that Saturday afternoon. Poor Trevor had been subjected to the "unkindest cut of all", as Mr. Perrigo called it, and was at home with Jerry's mom, wearing the "Cone of Shame".

The radio was on as usual, the volume knob turned all the way to the max. The three boys—Jerry, Kevin Kilgore, and Mike Perry—bobbed and swayed to Buddy Holly's "Peggy Sue", followed by "Great Balls of Fire" by Jerry Lee Lewis, which Kevin's mom claimed was downright filthy, if you listened to the words just right. When the songs petered out, a commercial praised the manly miracle of Brylcreem Hair Cream. Then yet another news bulletin blared through the Chevy's speaker; the sixth they'd heard that morning.

"Oh hell!" said Mr. Perrigo. "It's those damned sinkholes again!"

Atomic Arachnid Armageddon!

Kevin and Mike giggled and elbowed each other. Jerry's ears blazed crimson with embarrassment. "Dad! What would Mom say!"

The man—a bombastic Chevrolet dealership salesman by trade—grinned slyly. "She would undoubtedly warn me to watch my language in front of the boys," he said. "But, since she *isn't* here, I'll curse until I turn blue, if I have a mind to."

The newscaster, Edward R. Murrow from the authoritative sound of his voice, reported yet another "mysterious and inexplicable" sinkhole, this one appearing in the middle of the intersection of 14th Street and Jefferson in downtown Toledo, Ohio.

"Sinkhole!" snorted George Perrigo in disgust. "My grandfather had a ten-foot sinkhole open up behind his chicken coop way back in 1939 and no one made a big deal about that! Here it is, 1958, and everyone thinks the world is coming to an end!"

"Dad, these sinkholes are three hundred feet in diameter," Jerry told him. "And this makes fifty-two that have opened up in the last three days, all over the world. They make Grandpa's sinkhole look about as big as my butthole!"

Kevin and Mike thought that was hilarious. "You mean, the crater of Uranus, don't you?" asked Kevin, following up with that annoying mule bray of a laugh of his.

Mike quelled his amusement long enough to offer his opinion of the worldwide phenomenon. "I think they are holes that reach clear to the core of the earth, if you ask me."

"You dipstick!" said Jerry, rolling his eyes. "There would be boiling hot lava spewing out of the holes, if that was the case. The earth would be burned to a cinder in a matter of only a few hours."

"Better save your discussion for later, boys," suggested Mr. Perrigo. "You have now arrived at the premiere."

And so they had. The three hopped out of the back of the Chevy, onto the sidewalk in front of the Limelight Theater. They grinned in excited anticipation as they read the marquee out front.

It was a double-feature matinee. VAMPIRE ZOMBIES FROM OUTER SPACE and ATOMIC ARACHNID ARMAGEDDON.

Mr. Perrigo checked his trusty Timex. "It is now eleven o'clock AM," he calculated. "Both movies, plus intermission, adds up to a grand total of three hours and five minutes. I shall return several minutes prior to the ending credits for your luxuriant, chauffeured ride home."

"Thank you, Jeeves," said Jerry, giving his friends a wink.

Mr. Perrigo fished three dollar bills from his shirt pocket. "There you go, my boys. A movie ticket, a big popcorn and soft drink, and a box of Jujubes or Raisinets on me."

"Wow!" the boys said gratefully, each taking a crisp Washington. "Thanks a lot!"

As Mr. Perrigo drove away, to run errands at Western Auto and Sears & Roebuck, the three paid for their admission, then entered the lobby. They went to "water the petunias"—another George Perrigo saying—in the Men's room, then went straight to the concession stand.

"Boy, I've been wanting to see these two movies since I saw the previews!" said Kevin. "Vampires, zombies, aliens, and gargantuan invading spiders... all in the span of three hours! It's gonna be swell!"

"Actually," said Jerry, "the vampires and zombies are one and the same, thus VAMPIRE ZOMBIES FROM OUTER SPACE."

"But, if they're from outer space that would make them Vampire-Zombie-Aliens, wouldn't it?" countered Mike.

"That still doesn't make sense," Kevin said, putting his two cents worth in. "Zombies can't be vampires... their mouths are sewed-shut. That's what voodoo legend says."

Their serious, in-depth debate ended when their turn came at the counter. Each boy ordered a large popcorn, a drink, and a box of candy. Jerry chose Coca Cola and chocolate-covered Goobers,

Atomic Arachnid Armageddon!

Kevin a Dr. Pepper and Junior Mints, and Mike a 7-UP and fruity Mike & Ikes.

The three gave their tickets to the acne-ridden attendant at the auditorium entrance, received their stubs, and then climbed the stairs to the balcony. They found a trio of prime seats in the front row, where they could lean off the edge and toss unpopped corn kernels down the collars of unwary moviegoers, if the monster flicks didn't hold up to the hype and they got bored.

The theater lights dimmed and several previews lit up the screen. Upcoming features like THE TINGLER with Vincent Price, ALLIGATOR PEOPLE with Lon Chaney Jr., and THE GIANT GILA MONSTER with no big stars at all, but one really cool oversized lizard. A last call for refreshments followed with cartoon snacks prancing and dancing across the screen. Then the first feature began.

VAMPIRE ZOMBIES FROM OUTER SPACE starred John Ager, Sally Fraser, and Tor Johnson. The boys watched intently as flying saucers landed on the outskirts of New York City, depositing legions of vampire-zombies, their portly leader being the former-wrestler Tor. Ager and Fraser finally defeated the invaders with a sonic disrupter that disintegrated the monsters and saved the Earth from imminent destruction.

A ten-minute admission followed. Jerry and the others placed their drinks and popcorn in their seats, then loped down the stairs to take a quick pee. As they crossed the lobby, they overheard the manager and the concession stand girl talking about recent reports of giant sinkholes opening up in Chicago, Paris, and Tokyo within the past forty-five minutes. Jerry knew his dad was probably in the yard and lawn section at Sears at that very moment, test-kicking the tires of push mowers and complaining to a department store salesman about everyone getting their "tail feathers ruffled" about a few stupid sinkholes.

Soon, the three were back in their seats and the second feature began to roll. ATOMIC ARACHNID ARMAGEDDON starred Grant Williams, John Carradine, Yvonne DeCarlo, and Leo G. Carroll. In this movie, the ill-fated testing of an atomic bomb in the New Mexico desert radiated an underground nest of tarantulas, turning them into fifty foot monster spiders. The US Army attempted to destroy the marauding arachnids, but were sorrowfully defeated.

Halfway through the film, the ground beneath the theater seemed to rumble and shake.

"What was that?" asked Kevin, startled. "An earthquake?"

"In Louisville, Kentucky?" replied Jerry. "Quiet down and watch the movie, will you?"

As the feature continued, cities and towns across the United States were devastated by the giant arachnids, until Williams and Carroll developed a dozen death rays and mounted it on a squadron of jet fighters. The ray killed the giant spiders, sapping their radio-active powers and shriveling them to their former size.

As THE END blazed on the big screen and the house lights went up, Jerry and his friends deposited their litter in the trash receptacles and made their way downstairs.

"Pretty good," said Mike. "I still liked 20 MILLION MILES TO EARTH and THE MONOLITH MONSTERS better, though."

Jerry looked at his pal like he was nuts. "MONOLITH MONSTERS? Are you serious? Giant Magic Rocks, that's all they were. The Ymir in 20 MILLION MILES was pretty great, I'll admit that."

When the three stepped into the lobby, they knew something weird was going on... mostly because a big '55 Buick Skylark with white-wall tires came crashing through the front of the theater, taking out the ticket booth, the manager, and the concession stand in a matter of seconds.

Atomic Arachnid Armageddon!

They stood there, frozen to the spot for a moment, as broken glass and screams of terror filled the air. Then their boyish curiously got the better of them. "Let's see what's going on!" suggested Jerry. He headed through the open wall of the movie theater, his cohorts close at his heels.

The street out front was in complete chaos. While they were watching the final movie of the double-feature, a giant sinkhole had opened in the middle of Maple Avenue. And, from that deep, dark crater, swarmed an army of giant spiders. Not hairy magnified tarantulas like the ones in the last movie, but colossal black widows a good seventy feet in length and thirty feet in height. They were wreaking havoc, devouring citizens, and destroying private and public property at an alarming rate.

The boys couldn't help but be both surprised and secretly delighted. "Wow," said Mike in wonder. "It really is an Atomic Arachnid Armageddon! In the ever-loving spider flesh!"

"Yeah," said Kevin. "Who would've ever thunk it?"

Jerry was saddened to see one particularly mammoth widow rip his father's prized two-toned Chevy completely in half, then grind a shrieking George Perrigo between its razor-sharp mandibles.

"Poor Mr. Perrigo," said Kevin, placing a comforting hand on his friend's shoulder. "Sorry about that, buddy."

"Yeah," said Jerry, stunned. "What a bummer." He wondered what Mom would have to say about this.

Mike spotted the body of a National Guardsman lying in a pool of blood nearby, whose head had been bitten clean off the stub of his neck. He pulled an M14 rifle from the soldier's stiffening fingers and released a barrage of 7.62-millimeter rounds. "I've got dibs on Grant Williams," he said, spraying the approaching spiders with flying lead. Looking up at an angry black widow, Mike felt like the actor of his choice, but rather in the man versus spider battle in THE INCREDIBLE SHRINKING MAN.

"I'll take Carradine," said Kevin. He found a fragmentation grenade nearby, pulled the pin, and heaved it at an eight-legged monster attacking a Greyhound bus. It detonated a moment later, sending spider chunks and dismembered legs spinning.

"Okay," said Jerry, a little disappointed. "I'll be ugly old Leo G. Carroll. But you guys are going to have cover me until we can get to Dad's garage. He has enough junk and spare parts in there... I know I can build one humongous bastard of a death ray!"

His pals looked at him, surprised and impressed at the same time. Sure, he'd used profanity. But his mom wasn't there to scold him and, besides, as General William Tecumseh Sherman had once said in the face of adversity, "War is Hell!"... especially where a genuine, honest-to-goodness Atomic Arachnid Armageddon was concerned.

Cell Number Nine

Allen Cortez thought his eyes were playing tricks on him when he saw the spider crawl between the patient's liver and pancreas.

The tall, middle-aged surgeon looked up at those who assisted him. Mark Hurd, the anesthesiologist, was staring at him from the head of the operation gurney. He regarded the doctor with an expression between confusion and alarm. "Allen, did you see...?"

"Yes," he said. "Did anyone else?"

"Well, I thought I saw something," said Nurse Kristie Petrie, "but I couldn't be sure."

"See what?" asked Dr. Don Minor, a semi-retired surgeon who was assisting with the emergency surgery.

"A spider," Allen told him. Just saying it out loud made him feel incredibly foolish.

"*Spider*? You must be kidding! How did it get there... *inside* him?"

The nurse looked at the bank of halogen lights overhead. "Maybe it fell off the lights...you know, down into him." Although her lower face was covered, they could tell that she was frowning in disgust at the mere thought of it.

Allen said nothing, just kept operating. Probing through the framework of the Omni retractor, he meticulously extracted shotgun pellet from the bloody ruins of the man's gunshot stomach and upper intestines. No, despite Nurse Petrie's suggestion, he was certain that wasn't what had happened. Strangely, from the fleeting glimpse, it looked like the spider was accustomed to dwelling amid the internal organs of the criminal's abdomen...almost as though it was at home there.

"I wouldn't doubt that this jerk would be full of spiders and other nasty stuff," said a scrub tech named Ed, "considering what he pulled today."

Allen was aware of what he was referring to. The man they operated on had been injured during a convenience store robbery. Before the police had arrived, he had murdered seven people: the store owner and his wife, two adolescent boys who had been browsing through the comic book rack, a businessman who had stopped on his way home for a gallon of milk, and a woman who had been eight and a half months pregnant, walking through the door to pay for the gas she intended to pump into her mini-van. He was leaving the store when the cops showed up and a gunfight ensued. The killer wounded two officers before a third put a blast of double-aught buckshot point-blank into his belly. He had been hanging on by a thread when the EMTs brought him into the emergency of San Antonio Memorial.

"We're not here to pass judgement," Allen stated. He extracted another pellet and dropped it into a metal pan with a loud *clank*. "We're here to do our jobs to the best of our ability. We'll let the courts decide the appropriate punishment after we save his life."

The others said nothing, knowing in theory that Cortez was right. But their dedication to the Hippocratic Oath did little to dampen the contempt they felt toward the man on the table.

The surgeon took a stainless-steel instrument and carefully pulled the liver and pancreas away from one another, revealing the narrow recess in between. At first, he could see nothing amid the tremendous amount of blood that pooled there. "Suction, please."

Cell Number Nine

Petrie stepped forward and deftly cleared it for him. Instantly he saw the spider. It was nestled deeply in the tissue underneath. Allen caught it firmly between the tines of his surgical tweezers and attempted to extract the eight-legged parasite. The spider held fast, clinging to the viscera with the tenacity of a bulldog. Then, reluctantly, it lost its hold. Allen held it aloft. The surgical team stared at the spider, which was roughly the size of a quarter, jet black with a peculiar blue sheen to its glossy body and legs. It wiggled and squirmed in the tweezers' grasp, trying its best to escape.

"Bizarre," said Dr. Minor.

"Surreal is more like it," Allen replied. "Why and how it would be living inside this man's abdominal cavity is beyond me."

The others nodded in agreement.

Nurse Petrie opened a clear plastic vial and Allen carefully deposited the spider into its recess. It nearly scrambled free before she could screw the cap on. It fought furiously, clearly enraged, scratching at the transparent walls, leaving bloody streaks along the inside.

"What do you intend to do with it?"

"We'll send it down to Ted Maxwell in the lab," Allen told her. "He's something of a bug buff. Besides, he lives for mysteries like this."

Suddenly, the digital display on the heart monitor went haywire. The patient's blood pressure and pulse rate dropped dramatically and, abruptly, he flat-lined. "He's going into cardiac arrest."

Allen and his team attempted to resuscitate the criminal, but nothing worked; defibrillation, administering oxygen with an Ambu bag, even generous injections of Epinephrine…all failed to jump-start his heart and return it to its proper rhythm. After eighteen minutes, they finally ceased their efforts. They pronounced him dead at 7:53 PM.

"I can't say that I'm too upset about it," voiced Ed the tech. "They said that store was a real bloodbath."

Allen Cortez nodded solemnly and then left the operating room to clean up. The spider he had discovered in the man's torso still rattled him. Its extraction had seemed to have instigated the patient's death, almost as though the separation of the two had been the sole cause of the fatality.

Allen was leaving the hospital later that night, when someone called to him from the far side of the parking lot.

"Dr. Cortez! Wait up!"

He turned to find Sam Melford walking toward him. Melford was a veteran detective on the San Antonio police force. Detective Melford was short and stocky, with a shock of iron gray hair. He always appeared rumpled and weary, as though overworked to exhaustion or suffering from a severe case of insomnia.

"Hey, Sam," Allen replied. He slowed his pace, allowing the cop to catch up. "What can I do for you?"

"I hear you operated on James Lee Stapleton today," he said when he finally reached the doctor.

Allen frowned. "I'm sorry, but I can't place the name…"

"The guy who gunned down those people at the convenience store."

"Oh…him." Allen would have been happy to have put the man and the circumstances of his surgery completely from his mind, but apparently Detective Melford had no intention of allowing him to do so. "Mr. Stapleton didn't make it. He died on the table."

"Yes, I heard." Sam Melford stood there for a moment, seeming antsy and uncomfortable. "Uh, Doc, could you tell me one thing? When you were rooting around inside the guy, did you...well, did you find anything out of the ordinary? Something that shouldn't have been there?"

Allen felt an unsettling sensation grip him; a feeling that he could only describe as dread. "Like what?"

"Like *this*." The police detective reached inside his jacket and produced a small vial filled with alcohol. Floating inside was a shiny black spider identical to the one he had pulled from between the internal organs of James Lee Stapleton.

Although he had successfully concealed his distaste for spiders in the operating room, he couldn't help but take a wary step backward at that moment. If the physician had a fear of anything, it was spiders. The phobia had stemmed from his childhood. When he was a young boy, probably six or seven-years-old, he had lived in a mobile home. Just outside his bedroom window, a large garden spider had built a massive web. His mother assured him that it was harmless, but it had seemed so wicked and predatory, trapping all manner of flies and small insects in its silken strands, that all he saw was pure evil in the arachnid. As a result of its presence, he suffered many dark and disturbing nightmares. Allen thought he would have outgrown the childish fear, but that had not been the case. Interestingly, he could read about spiders, watch television programs about them, and even view them in zoo exhibits behind plate glass, but if they were out in the open and near enough to touch, the old anxiety and terror kicked in. He absolutely hated spiders; there was no two ways about it.

Upon seeing the spider in the plastic vial, he was tempted to deny that he had seen anything like it. But he had known Sam for years and had assisted him with medical knowledge on numerous cases. It seemed unthinkable to attempt to pull the wool over his eyes now. Besides, the veteran cop would see him for a liar the moment the denial crossed his lips.

Allen sighed. "Yes, I did. I found one exactly like that...inside the patient."

"Exactly where inside him?" Sam wanted to know.

"In his abdominal cavity. Between his liver and pancreas." He studied the detective with interest. "Exactly where did you get that specimen?"

"I'm not at liberty to discuss that right now. But I will say one thing. This isn't the first one to cross my desk."

"There have been others? With spiders inside them?"

"All violent criminals who have done hideous, unthinkable things," the cop admitted. "But, like I said, I can't elaborate at this time."

Allen recalled several cases that had graced the local headlines during the past few months. A man who had slaughtered his entire family—wife and three young children—before turning the gun on himself. A man who had walked into a McDonald's and gunned down twelve people in cold blood before SWAT had brought him down with a sniper bullet. A couple more, too, each more gruesome and bloodier than the one before.

"What's going on, Sam?" Allen asked him. "And what does this have to do with spiders?"

Detective Melford looked like he wanted to give the surgeon the same song-and-dance as before, but since they had a history and had possessed something of a professional relationship for several years, he let his guard down. "Just let me say that, prior to today's incident, James Lee Stapleton was nothing more than a small-time criminal. One with a rap sheet as long as your arm, mind you, but all of them borderline petty crimes. Bad checks, marijuana possession, one case of grand theft auto when he was in his early twenties. But nothing overtly violent...not in the least. His record pegged him as nothing more than a lazy bum who wouldn't hurt a fly."

"So, if that was the case, why did he kill seven innocent people at that store?"

"We have no earthly idea. The security camera showed that the owner was cooperating. He gave Stapleton the cash with no resistance whatsoever. But then the crook got this look in his eyes; a flat-out mean, mad-dog look. After that he just started shooting everyone in the joint. He even reloaded to finish off the last few victims."

"I'm no psychiatrist," admitted Allen, "but that does sound peculiar. And the others?"

"The same as Stapleton. Basically, harmless career criminals who just snapped and went kill crazy. One wasn't even a criminal at all, just an eighteen-year-old kid who was in the joint for a couple of days for failing to pay his speeding tickets."

"And they all had this…this type of *spider*… inside them?"

"Yes. And they would have remained hidden and undetected, if they hadn't been revealed by surgery or autopsy."

"It just keeps getting curiouser and curiouser," Allen said, quoting Alice from her adventures in Wonderland.

"You better believe it," agreed Sam. "Just promise me this, Doc. If you operate on anyone else and come across another one of these ugly little buggers…will you give me a call?"

"Of course," Allen promised. "Immediately."

"Thanks," replied the cop. He placed the specimen back into his coat pocket, out of sight, much to the surgeon's relief. "I have a theory about what's going on here, but it's so damned convoluted and bizarre, the Chief would rake me over the coals if I was one iota wrong about the whole deal. I need every bit of evidence I can get before taking steps to wrap up this stream of blood-thirsty homicides."

"Well, when you finally reach that point, please, don't keep me in the dark," Allen told him. "I'd really like to know what motivated these guys to do what they did…as well as exactly why they were walking around with a spider scurrying around inside them."

Detective Melford nodded. "Will do, Doc. You'll be the first one I call."

Then the San Antonio policeman was crossing the parking lot to his unmarked car, leaving the Texas surgeon feeling more than a little intrigued—and uneasy—about the strange conversation he had just taken part in.

Three days later, Allen Cortez was stepping out of an elevator, when Eldan Eichbaum approached him. The neurosurgeon seemed in a hurry. "Ah, Allen, just the man I was looking for."

"What's the problem, Eldan?" he asked.

"Are you available to assist me with emergency surgery? A man was just brought in. The police said that he tried to commit suicide." A disturbed expression crossed Eichbaum's face. "I heard that he killed his family and…well, he *cannibalized* them. A neighbor complained of the stench coming from his apartment and the authorities investigated. Apparently, he thought death would be a better option than life imprisonment."

A sensation of déjà vu gripped Cortez. The Stapleton surgery instantly came to mind. He wanted to decline Eichbaum's invitation to participate in the procedure, but his morbid curiosity wouldn't allow him to. "Yes, of course. I'll be glad to assist."

Cell Number Nine

Fifteen minutes later they were dressed in scrubs and sterilized for surgery. Several members of Allen's surgical team were present; anesthesiologist Mark Hurd and Ed the tech, to name a couple. The assisting nurse was Ann Hurd, Mark's wife.

The man, an African-American in his mid-forties, had put a nine-millimeter through his right temple. The slug had passed through the lateral ventricle, traveling upward in a diagonal path, and lodging in the center of the cerebrum. He was still alive, but he was unconscious, and his vital signs were weakening by the moment.

Allen assisted Dr. Eichbaum as he made the initial incisions, lifting away the flesh of the scalp and, referring to the images of a CAT-scan on an overhead monitor, sawed a fragment of the man's skull away, revealing the brain within. It was swollen and strangely discolored, appearing dark and bruised.

"This is odd," stated the neurosurgeon. "Very odd indeed."

Allen said nothing. To him, it wasn't very odd at all. He leaned forward, examining the wrinkled folds of the patient's discolored cerebrum.

"What are you looking for, Allen?" Eldan asked him after a moment.

"*That*," he said.

He could tell that Dr. Eichbaum was startled by the discovery he had made. Clinging to the tissue of the brain was not one blue-black spider, but three. They seemed to pulsate, as though feeding off the circulation of the cranial organ. But, no, on further inspection, Allen surmised that the opposite was taking place. Somehow, the spiders were delivering rather than taking, as though pumping minute amounts of some dark and nasty poison into the man's diseased brain.

"What...what is this?" Dr. Eichbaum stepped backward, looking a bit disoriented.

"It's those damned spiders again, isn't it?" asked Hurd.

"Yes," said Allen in scarcely a whisper. "Three this time." A disturbing thought suddenly came to mind. If there were three spiders in this poor man's brain, then how many more could be elsewhere in his anatomy, scurrying through muscle and tissue, along bone and through vascular arteries?

Eichbaum looked at his assisting surgeon. "I heard the story through the grapevine, Allen, but I had no idea that it was actually true. Are these similar to the one you found?"

"Identical," Allen told him, his throat feeling dry and parched. He glanced over at the nurse. "Ann, bring me something to deposit these... *things* ...in."

Soon, she had brought a container with multiple chambers for storing various tissues during exploratory biopsies. Allen attempted to extract the first spider, but his hand trembled so violently that he found it impossible. He looked the neurosurgeon squarely in the eyes. "Do you mind?"

Eldan Eichbaum nodded in understanding and went to work with the calm and precision that made him the best in his chosen field. With some effort, he pried the trio of arachnids from the bloated tissue of the brain and dropped them into the individual compartments of the biopsy container. The spiders scrambled and clawed frantically, attempting to escape. But the hinged lids of the chambers remained tightly in place.

Allen almost held his breath in anticipation of what was to come next. It happened thirty seconds later. The patient went into Code Blue. His brain and pulmonary rhythms spiked violently, then flat-lined the same way James Lee Stapleton had done.

The doctors did everything possible to spare the man's life, but nothing worked. The patient was dead and there was no chance of bringing him back to stand trial for the atrocities he had performed.

Or was *forced* to perform, thought Allen. He knew the thought was foolish and unorthodox for a man of science like himself. But, deep down inside, he was a hundred percent certain that it was absolutely true.

When he got back to his office, Allen Cortez called Ted Maxwell at the lab.

"I haven't been able to identify this ugly little spider you sent to me," Maxwell told him. "I've taken photos and emailed them to several top arachnologists in the country and none have seen anything remotely similar before. If I could take it out and pin it down on a specimen board, maybe I could find some identifying marks on its back or underbelly that might help narrow down its origins and sub-genre."

"No!" protested Allen. "Whatever you do...don't release the thing!"

"I'm way ahead of you, doctor," Maxwell replied. "I've done some research on the internet concerning parasitic arachnids and came across one bit of antiquated information that is pretty intriguing. Here, I'm emailing it to you right now."

A few seconds later, the email showed up in Allen's inbox. He brought up the file that Maxwell had attached. It was a photocopy of a yellowed page from an old diary or journal, written in the strong, bold hand of a man.

Sheriff's journal, April 22nd, 1884

The new jail was finally finished today. Now the God-fearing folks of Cotulla will be safe from undesirables and those generally up to no good. Behind my office is a separate block of nine jail cells... four on either side of a passageway with the ninth located at the very end. The bars are forged of iron, fashioned by the local blacksmith, and the doors are equipped with modern, flat-key locks.

I should feel more at ease with this new jail completed. It certainly is much better than the two-celled jail that I was accustomed to before. But, oddly enough, all that I feel is a nagging sense of unease. Most of that unease comes from cell Number Nine. It appears identical to all the others in dimension and construction, except for one detail. There is a single stone set in the southern wall of the cell that is unlike any of the others. Truthfully, it is not a stone at all, but more like a large chunk of quartz or transparent glass. It is amber in color and contains something trapped inside.

The thing inside that chunk of orange glass is a large spider about half as big as my hand. But that isn't all. Behind it is something even larger, dark and egg-shaped. It almost looks like a nest of some kind...

Allen's eyes moved downward to a second entry.

Sheriff's journal, July 9th, 1884
Big John Alder is screaming in Cell Number Nine, rattling the bars, pleading for us to put him down like a rabid dog in the street.

This is not the man I've dealt with on a regular basis for the past three years. Big John was always a quiet and cunning man of a particularly shady nature. You could never tell what was going on behind that stone-still face of his or behind those cold gray eyes. A thousand hardened men would lose their nerve before Big John would even consider breaking a sweat. But today his last nerve is lost and he is screaming like a frightened child begging for his mother.

Big John has done something to that amber stone in the wall. Maybe he was trying to tunnel through the wall or was simply being destructive in that senseless way of his. Whatever the reason, he has cracked the thing open and the spider inside is gone. I've searched the ninth cell myself, thoroughly, but found nothing.

Big John claims that it is inside him.

If he continues to rant and scream the way he has for the past few hours, I may make good on his suggestion and put a bullet from my Colt between his frightened eyes...

Then a third and final entry, hastily scribbled and disjointed.

Sheriff's journal, October 30th, 1884

Cell Number Nine

Oh God, take me now! Squash me like the maggot I am with your mighty hand.

Big John was right. It gets inside and roams around and around… like Satan in the Book of Job… walking up and down… to and fro.

I feel it in me now…twisting my thoughts… making it hard to think.

Those bastards and bitches in town…laughing at me… laughing at my pain and fear. I'll show them, though. They'll feel my agony and terror tenfold… and then they will feel no more…

The journal entries chilled Allen Cortez to the bone.

"See what I mean?" asked Maxwell over the phone. "Scary stuff, huh?"

"Yes," answered Allen. "More than you know. Thanks, Ted. This has been extremely helpful."

After his conversation with the lab technician, Allen sat in his chair for several minutes, wrestling with what course to take next. It didn't take long. He typed a quick email to Detective Melford at the San Antonio Police Department, attached the file Maxwell had sent him, and sent the message. Then he picked up the phone and dialed Melford's number.

A second later, a familiar voice answered. "Hello? Melford here."

"Check your inbox, Sam. I sent you a message…along with something else."

Allen sat and listened as the distant sound of fingers tapping on a keyboard echoed over the line. There was a long stretch of silence before Sam Melford spoke again.

"Damn."

"Sam, the men responsible for all these killings…did they have a connection to the place mentioned in the journal? Cotulla?"

The detective sighed heavily. "Yes…all of them were incarcerated in the Cotulla jail…shortly before it was condemned."

"Condemned?"

"Yes, the old jail became too dangerous. A new one was built and opened eight months ago. James Lee Stapleton and a dozen others were the last to serve time in the old jail before it was shut down."

"And the cell they occupied?"

"Was Number Nine," Sam told him grimly. "According to La Salle County public records."

A long, awkward silence stretched across the phone line for the better part of thirty seconds. Then Allen spoke. "So, what are you going to do, Sam?"

"I think I'll drive down to Cotulla and take a look around for myself. I don't suppose you'd like to go with me, would you?"

"As a matter of fact, my surgery schedule is clear tomorrow."

"Great. I'll pick you up around seven. We'll grab a bite of breakfast, then hit the road."

"That sounds fine."

Sam Melford said nothing else, just hung up the phone.

Allen sat back in his chair and considered the mystery of the parasitic spiders and the role he had played in it up to that point. He had to admit; he was scared shitless. He would have liked nothing better than to have stayed put in San Antonio and forgotten the whole sorry situation.

But once again, his blasted curiosity got the better of him and he knew that he had no other choice but to go and face his fears, whether they were foolish and unfounded, or otherwise.

It took them an hour and half to drive the 89 miles from San Antonio to the little Texas oil town of Cotulla. They arrived around

Cell Number Nine

nine thirty and had to stop a couple of times for directions before they found the place they had come to see.

The old jail was located on a rundown side of town, surrounded by abandoned stores and cracked sidewalks choked with weeds and discarded litter. Sam parked his car outside and the two sat there for a long moment, studying the building. It was ancient; a one-story adobe structure common in West Texas, New Mexico, and Arizona in the mid to late 1800s. The panes of the front window were shattered. The remaining shards of the glass reflected in the bright sunlight, while the shadows of the interior were dense and murky.

Sam and Allen looked at one another. "Well, we're here," said the detective. "Might as well go in and see if we can find anything."

Allen simply nodded, although he dreaded setting foot in the place, given its disturbing history. The doctor began to wonder why he had agreed to tag along in the first place.

They left the car and crossed the covered walkway to the front door. They expected it to be locked, but it wasn't. The heavy wooden door swung inward with a squeal of rusty iron hinges.

The darkness beyond the threshold was ominous, to say the least. "Wait a second." Sam returned to his car and retrieved a heavy, black Maglite. The flashlight cast a beam that cut through the gloom, revealing mounds of garbage and broken furniture. As they walked inside, Sam swept the beam from side to side. In a far corner was an old mattress surrounded by discarded cans and empty beer bottles. "Looks like someone's been living here. Maybe just a homeless guy passing through."

"Where are the cells?" Allen asked him. His voice sounded loud and hollow in the front room of the abandoned jail.

Sam indicated a door behind a long, wooden counter. "Back there, I suppose." The policeman hesitated and looked at the surgeon steadily. "I don't know what we'll find back there, but considering what's happened in the past few days, I believe we must be prepared for anything." Sam pulled back the right side of his jacket, revealing a holstered .38. "And I mean *anything*."

Together, they entered the doorway. At first there was a narrow hallway with small rooms on both sides that had once been used as makeshift offices. Then another door confronted them, standing partially open. It was heavier than the other with a small barred window in the upper panel and an old box-style lock below the handle.

Sam pushed the door open and they found themselves in the cellblock of the old jail. Four cells stretched to their left and another four to their right. Further on, stood Cell Number Nine. Its iron bars were corroded with age and laced with tatters of old cobwebs. Unlike the doors of the other eight cells, the door of Number Nine stood open, as though inviting them inside.

"Do you think it's still there?" asked Allen. Goosebumps prickled the flesh of his arms as they walked across the cobbled floor toward the cell at the end of the corridor. "You know...the amber stone in the wall?"

"That's what we're about to find out." Sam took the lead. They stepped through the open doorway of the jail cell and studied the interior in the glow of the battery-powered light. It was sparse in furnishings: only a single bunk against the left wall and a filthy sink and commode to the right, obviously added sometime after the turn of the century. The room had a dank, mildewed odor to it, along with another mixture of scents that both men were grimly familiar with. The coppery smell of congealed blood and the decay of human flesh.

"That stench," said Allen. "Where is it coming from?"

Sam turned the beam of his flashlight in a slow circle until it revealed something they had not seen a moment before. "There. Beneath the bunk."

They crouched and found the source of the nasty odor. It was the body of a man. The corpse lay on its side, its clothing stained with dried blood in a dozen places. The body was sunken and emaciated, like that of a mummy.

"What the hell happened to this guy, Doc?"

Taking the flashlight, Allen examined the remains. "It looks like his bodily fluids were siphoned, the way a...a spider drains an insect of its life's blood."

"How long has he been there?"

"For several weeks I'd say. Maybe longer. It's difficult to tell with tissue degeneration of this severity."

Melford shook his head. "It almost looks like he scrambled under there to hide. To get away from something."

Together, they turned toward the back wall of the cramped cell. When the beam of the Maglite illuminated the stone and mortar, one feature in the very center was immediately apparent. A rectangular block gleaming like amber glass in the glow of the flashlight.

"That's it," said Sam.

They studied it without getting too close. The rock was split in half, revealing a deep crater in the center. Sam extended his light. The inner recess of the amber block was empty. No large spider and no egg-shaped nest like those described in the sheriff's journal. Just a pocket of nothing.

"They're not there," came an unexpected voice from behind. "But they're around."

They turned to find a man standing on the other side of the cell doorway. He was tall and lean, his hair thinning to the point of transparency and his face gaunt and unshaven. He was dressed in a deputy's uniform that had once been crisp khaki but was now wrinkled and darkly stained with sweat and other fluids of a more sinister nature. The badge above his right-hand pocket was tarnished and dull, and the embroidered patch on his upper sleeves identified him as an officer of the Cotulla Police Department.

He looked to be beyond exhaustion and his eyes belied an unstable mentality. A crooked grin crossed his thin face and he winked. "Oh, they're most definitely around here somewhere."

"Who are you?" asked Sam calmly.

"It doesn't matter anymore," the man muttered. "Someone who couldn't bear to let go, I reckon. Why the hell would I want to move onward, to a nice cushy job in that spanking brand-new jailhouse...when all my little friends are right here where they belong? Where I belong?"

"You worked here?" asked Allen.

"Worked here?" The idea seemed to amuse the man and he expelled a coarse, phlegmy laugh. "Maybe at first. Then they made themselves known to me and I merely existed. I shunned my family and friends...my humanity. Nothing mattered...but to serve them."

"And by serving them, you mean... him?" asked the police detective, pointing to the dried remains beneath the bunk.

The deputy shrugged his narrow shoulders. "Some they dominate, others they devour. He was one of the lucky ones."

"Exactly who are they?" Allen wanted to know.

The man glared at him. "You know who they are! I can see it in your eyes. The spiders, man! The freaking spiders!"

Allen glanced over at Sam and noticed that his attention had been glued to one particular point during the course of the conversation. The surgeon followed his gaze and suddenly felt his heart skip a beat.

The deputy's hand was on the cell door. It wasn't immediately apparent though, whether his intention was to steady himself to keep from falling...or to slam the door shut, locking them securely inside.

Inside with the spiders.

Almost as if on cue. Allen detected movement in the cell around them. On the walls, the floor, the raftered ceiling overhead. Sam was aware of it at the same time. He lifted his flashlight to reveal the source.

"I wouldn't do that if I were you," the deputy warned. "They cherish the darkness. Light only pisses them off."

Allen recalled how the spiders had reacted beneath the brilliance of the halogen light in the operating room; angry and aggressive.

"I have no idea what their intentions will be toward you," he said as he began to swing the door slowly inward. "Maybe they'll suck you dry. Or maybe they'll take up residence deep down inside, nestled cozy and warm, in your guts, in your brain." His lean face twitched spasmodically. "For your sake, I hope they're hungrier than hell."

Without warning, Sam drew his revolver and aimed it at the man. "Stand perfectly still or I'll fire."

The deputy stared at the older gentleman incredulously. "You wouldn't shoot me, would you? A fellow brother of the law?"

"I'll kill you if you don't let go of that door...right now."

The man snickered cruelly "You don't call the shots, old man. They do." Then with a shove, he sent the door swinging inward.

At that instant, two things happened. Sam fired his .38, while Allen leapt forward. The deputy flailed backward and dropped to the floor of the outer corridor, a bullet hole dribbling blood just above his left eye. Allen knew from experience that the placement of the bullet had likely killed the man upon impact. The doctor reached the door and shoved his right hand between the iron door and the inner edge of the doorframe. The metal struck the doctor's knuckles, causing him to cry out...but at least the momentum of the heavy door had been halted.

Allen turned to see Sam returning the gun to its holster...and lifting the flashlight toward the rear of the cell.

"No!" he yelled, but it was too late.

The beam of light revealed thousands of small blue-black spiders identical to the ones he found inside the bodies of the two men he had performed surgery on. Like a black tide, they moved as a single entity, scrambling angrily across wood and stone. Making a violent, swirling beeline…straight for them.

"Run!" ordered Sam. Allen pushed the door open, but it rebounded as it struck the sole of the deputy's shoe. Frantically, he caught the door before it could clang shut. Shoving hard, he knocked the man's foot aside and leapt over his body. He began to sprint down the narrow corridor, toward the oak door that led to the office beyond.

He turned to make sure Sam was behind him. The detective was passing through the open doorway of the cell, when he tripped and fell across the body of the gunshot deputy. Sam screamed as a wave of darkness surged across the stone floor of the jail cell, covering his shoes, then his ankles.

Allen ran back and helped Sam to his feet, bending to brush several spiders from the detective's shoes and socks. Then, together, they ran through the cellblock door, past the tiny offices and the front room, and into bright, warm sunlight.

When they made it to the car, they caught their breath and watched the open door of the old jail. Thirty seconds passed, then a minute. It appeared that while the pale light of a flashlight infuriated the spiders, pure daylight horrified them. They remained inside, out of sight.

Allen looked over at his friend. "Sam…did they…?"

"No, I don't think so," the policeman told him, clearly shaken and struggling for breath. "I didn't feel anything."

For a long moment, they said nothing, just continued to watch the dark doorway of the condemned building. "So, what do we do now?" Allen asked.

Cell Number Nine

Sam said nothing. He simply walked to the rear of his car, popped the lid of the trunk, and lifted a five-gallon gas can from within. He unscrewed the cap and extended the collapsible spout.

Allen looked around, but that particular section of the little town of Cotulla was completely deserted. No one was around to see what was about to take place.

"Looks like you were more prepared than I thought," the doctor told him. "But...but shouldn't you contact the local authorities? You...you just shot a man and now you're torching the place? What you're doing... isn't this a crime?"

Sam regarded him with a mixture of irritation and disbelief. "I'd say a public service is more like it."

Allen remained beside the car as Sam circled the building several times, saturating the foundation and the dry weeds around it with gasoline. He took a book of matches from his coat pocket, lit one, and then pitched it at the ground. Flames blossomed as the fuel ignited. The fire progressed faster than they expected and, soon, the structure was fully engulfed.

Quickly, they jumped into the car and made their escape. They took a route opposite of the way they had arrived. As they crossed the city limits, they could hear sirens in the distance and see the dark billow of smoke in the rear-view mirror.

Allen looked over at Sam. The police detective clutched the steering wheel tightly, his face pensive "Sam, are you sure...?"

"I'm okay, Allen. I promise." The cop took a deep breath and sighed. "Now let's go home and forget that this whole nasty business ever took place."

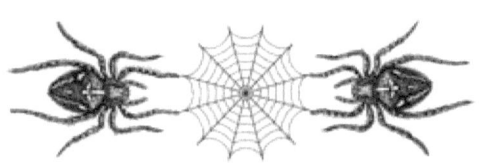

Several weeks had passed since the incident at Cotulla.

Some nights, Allen Cortez would awaken in the dead of night, hearing the clang of the cell door in his ears and feeling a thousand tiny bodies scurrying across his skin, first tickling, then skewering him with white-hot needles. He always sat up in bed, terrified, bathed in sweat, his breathing labored.

He had attempted to contact Sam Melford a dozen times, but the detective was never there. He was either out sick or was taking some personal time off. Allen left messages on the detective's voice mail, but they were never answered.

Toward the end of the month, Allen received a phone call from San Antonio Memorial's surgical coordinator.

"Dr. Cortez, I was checking to see if you could perform emergency surgery in, say, fifteen minutes or so?"

Allen swallowed dryly. "Sure. What's the urgency?"

"Multiple gunshot wounds," the coordinator told him. "There was a mass shooting at police headquarters downtown. Five officers were killed and four seriously injured."

"And the shooter...?"

"...will be the one you will be operating on." The woman at the other end of the line hesitated, then continued. "He's also a police officer."

Allen closed his eyes, his hand gripping the phone's receiver tightly. "You wouldn't happen to know his name, would you?"

"I'm afraid not. All I know is that he was a veteran cop. He had been with the force for nearly thirty-six years." There was a pause. "There's something you ought to know...if the stories that have been circulating around the hospital are true."

A cold dread threatened to overtake him. "What is that?"

"The police said that there were spiders around his body. Dozens of them."

Allen's heart hammered in his chest. "Did...they *catch* them?"

"Well...no. It was chaotic...they had a lot to deal with. I suppose they simply crawled away."

Allen sighed, attempting to calm himself. "Which operating room are you scheduling?"

"Number Nine," she told him.

Number Nine, he thought. *How tragically ironic.*

"I'll be there."

When he hung up the phone, he sat in his chair for several minutes, staring at a small plastic vial that stood beside his computer keyboard. Inside was a blue-black spider, curled up and suspended in alcohol.

Motionless and dead...unlike the others he was now aware of.

He recalled his question to his friend, as well as the answer that followed.

"Sam... did they...?"

"No, I don't think so. I didn't feel anything."

A cold dread threatened to overtake him. *"I bet you feel it now... don't you Sam?"*

Grimly, Allen Cortez left his office and headed downstairs to prepare for surgery.

The Creeping Sands

*S*he awoke and stared into total darkness.

It was peculiar not being able to see anything at all. Usually there was some sort of illumination; the glow of the alarm clock or a trace of nocturnal light beyond the bedroom window. But the black she encountered at that moment was complete and impenetrable.

She lay there and was aware of movement all around her. It wasn't something that she heard, but rather sensed. That was another disconcerting fact; the silence was as complete as the darkness. The sound of her husband's breathing next to her, the whistle of the wind around the eaves of the house, the barking of the neighbor's dog... none could be heard. Only quietness like the depths of a grave and that sensation of mass movement.

For a maddening moment, she simply lay there, afraid to even move. Then something brushed her face... a fine filament like the silky strand of a woman's hair. Then another... and yet another. She lifted her hand to her face and the strands clung to her fingers; sticky, difficult to discard. What's happening? she wondered. Curiosity turned into fright and fright into panic. What's going on?

Finally, she could wait no longer. She reached over and, fumbling for the switch of the nightstand lamp, turned it on.

Spiders. They were everywhere. Clinging to the ceiling in a dark, seething mat, coursing up the bedroom walls, collecting on the panes of the window, shutting out any trace of light from outside. They were all shapes, sizes, and colors; black, brown, and gray, some as small as the nail of her little finger, others as large as her entire hand.

The blanket of arachnids on the ceiling above her moved in tandem, seeming to scuttle over one another like the waves of a dark and restless ocean. She sensed the same motion around her and looked down to see more spiders traveling across the bedcovers, creeping slowly toward her. Their tiny eyes sparkled hungrily, their incisors moist, working to and fro, preparing for the bite.

It was at that moment that she looked upward and saw the ones on the ceiling descending on silken threads; slowly at first, then quickening, closing the gap between her and them.

And, a second before they converged, she opened her mouth and…

…screamed.

It was a second or two before Shona Marino realized that she had broken past the boundary of her nightmare and was vocally venting the horror it had conjured. She sat up in her bed, the shrill cry reaching its pinnacle, then fading in the back of her throat. Wildly, she looked around the dark bedroom. The window glowed with a trace of moonlight, while the electric alarm clock blazed 12:54 in bold red numbers.

Her husband, David, rolled onto his back with a groan. "Crickey, woman! Are you having that bloody nightmare again?"

Shona breathed in deeply, attempting to settle her nerves. "Sorry, luv, but it was a bad one this time. Not just a few of the little buggers, but hundreds, maybe thousands."

David shifted uneasily on the mattress. "Well, that's a comforting thought."

Suddenly, the bedroom light came on. They looked over to see their eleven-year-old daughter, Taylor, standing there with her hand on the light switch. "Is Mum dreaming about spiders again?" she asked sleepily.

"Afraid so, dear," Shona told her. "Sorry I frightened you. Go on back to bed now."

Taylor shook her head in disgust. "Want me to turn off the light?" she asked.

"No, leave it on," her mother replied. "I may read a bit."

The girl sighed and, zombie-like, shuffled down the hallway, heading back to her room.

"You'd better get some sleep," David advised her. "We do have our camping trip at Cooloola tomorrow. If you stay up half the night reading those ungodly horror books of yours, you'll end up being a holy terror."

Shona laughed. "What do you mean?"

"I mean, you'll be in a cranky mood and you'll bitch all weekend long. And then you and Taylor will butt heads and you'll both be bitching to beat the band, and me and Hayley will get caught in the middle and we'll all have a bloody miserable trip."

Shona's hand hovered over the Richard Laymon novel that lay on the nightstand next to the alarm clock, then withdrew. "Yes, I suppose you're right. I'll try to get back to sleep, but I'm not making any promises. Alright if I leave the light on a while longer?"

"If it makes you feel any better." David leaned over and gave her peck on the cheek. "You and your bloody spiders!"

Shona lay back down and closed her eyes. A moment later, she opened them and stared around the bedroom. The ceiling, the walls, the window… all were clear.

Get those confounded buggers out of your brain, girl! she told herself. Shona took a deep breath and settled into her pillow, trying to relax. At least she would have no such worries at Teewah Beach. The only spiders they were likely to see there were a few tree spiders in the wooded expanse of Cooloola Campground along the coastline. And you certainly wouldn't see any on the beach itself… a few stray crabs maybe, but no spiders.

The Creeping Sands

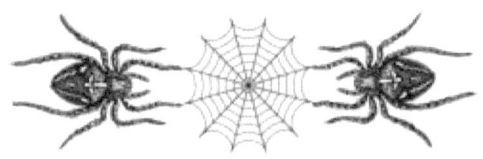

It was late Thursday evening when Shona Marino and her family finally finished setting up their campsite on a prime spot at Cooloola on the edge of the Great Sandy National Park. They had worked most of the afternoon, backing David's Toyota Landcruiser four-wheel-drive into position, unfolding their Jimboomba camper trailer, and putting everything properly into place. From beneath the canvas overhang, they had an excellent view of Teewah Beach on the Queensland coast of Australia, as well as the broad expanse of the Coral Sea just beyond.

As they began to wind down, Shona regarded herself and her family. Shona was in her early thirties, a brunette with an olive complexion that owed much to her father's French/Italian heritage. She was the Queensland Franchise Manager for Health Information Pharmacy Group out of Brisbane. Her job took her on the road alot, traveling from pharmacy to pharmacy. She was thankful that she had managed such a long weekend off; her job was so demanding that she rarely got off more than a couple of days at a time.

Her husband, David, was preparing dinner—roast pork and potatoes— in the kitchen area a few feet away. David was in his mid-thirties, with brown hair, blue eyes, and a goatee. Her husband was the easiest person to get along with. He could talk to anyone and everyone seemed to love him.

Shona's oldest daughter, Taylor, was eleven and like her in more ways than she could count. Taylor was tall for her age with light brown hair and big brown eyes. Taylor had a fiery side to her and she could be a bit moody sometimes. That, in turn, caused her and Shona to butt heads on occasion. They were both very stubborn and liked to have the last say. But all in all, Taylor could be very sensitive and quiet, especially around people she was unfamiliar with.

Her youngest daughter, Hayley, however, was the complete opposite of her sister. The eight-year-old was rambunctious and outgoing and loved to be the center of attention. Haley took after David's side of the family with mousy brown hair, blue eyes, and a liberal sprinkling of freckles on her light skin.

Shona smiled to herself and settled back in her camp chair, reading the Laymon book by the light of a battery-powered lamp. "Will dinner be long?" she asked David.

"The potatoes have ten or fifteen minutes to go and then they're done," he told her over his shoulder.

A peal of boisterous laughter drew Shona's attention from her reading. Annoyed, she glanced over to a neighboring campsite several yards away. A big, raw-boned Aussie and several of his mates were sitting around a campfire, drinking and trading tales. The main one of the bunch was the kind that most outsiders thought of when they pictured a true Australian man: burly and ruddy in the face, his features weathered, and sporting bristly mutton-chop sideburns. From the loudness and slight slur of his speech, Shona could tell that he had downed more than his share of lager that evening.

Shona tried to ignore the man and continue her reading, but found herself listening to him instead. "I swear to God, it's true, every last word of it!" bellowed the big man. He upended a bottle of Powers, drained it, and then reached into a cooler of ice for another. "My dear old dad told me the tale when I was just a lad!"

"Crickey!" scoffed one of the other fellows. "That bloody spider story is pure rubbish and that's all! Every schoolboy knows that!"

Shona perked up. *Spider? Did he say spider?*

The big man with the sideburns laughed loudly. "Well, I was never much of a schoolboy. I was out helping on my grandpap's fishing boat by the time I was eight. But you're wrong about the sea spiders, for I've seen 'em with my own bloody eyes!"

A younger fellow in his twenties sat on the other side of the campfire. "I've never heard this tale myself. Why don't you give it a once-over, George, if only for my sake?"

George unleashed a belch that rocked him from head to toe. "Don't mind if I do, Tommy!" He emptied his bottle of lager, but refrained from grabbing another as he began to spin the yarn. His twinkling blue eyes lost a bit of their merriment and suddenly turned serious. "The legend has been told across the length and breadth of Old Australia for nearly two hundred years, the same as I tell it tonight. They say a Spanish galleon somehow made its way across the Pacific, ending Down Under along this very coast. But it wasn't just any galleon, but a pirate ship that had looted the Spaniard's fleets and made off with a fortune in golden doubloons. Millions of dollars' worth it carried in the dark belly of its hold. The captain and crew had intentions of porting near Brisbane and settling down from their lives of piracy. But alas, it wasn't to be! A hellacious storm took the galleon down, sinking it. All hands were lost and the hull of the ship found itself on the bottom of the Coral Sea, its fortune hidden away in the cold, dark depths of the Big Blue.

"Well, for year upon year, Aussies traded the tale and some hungered for that lost gold. One such man was Pervy White, a treasure hunter if there ever was one. Back in '73, when I was a much younger lad, I was one of eight men who accompanied ol' Pervy on an expedition to locate that scuttled pirate galleon and its fortune in gold coin. He'd bought an old map at a swap meet and swore that it pinpointed the sunken ship's location to the very fathom. For weeks we searched, until a drag line brought up evidence that sent our spirits soaring; a barnacled board from the very galleon we were in search of. Pervy insisted on donning deep sea diving gear—you know, the old-style with the port-holed helmet and all—and retrieving the treasure himself. And that was exactly what he did!"

The young fellow named Tommy puffed excitedly on a Winfield Red as he listened. "Well, go on now! What happened next?"

"Pervy White clamped down his helmet, gave us a thumb's up, and we lowered him into the depths of Davy Jones' Locker. He gave us instructions to leave him down for twenty minutes and then bring him up. We did just that. But something went horribly wrong. Fifteen minutes into the dive, the oxygen gauge went haywire. It was as though Pervy's air hose had been severed somehow. I suppose we panicked then. We hoisted him up slowly, so as not to subject him to the bends. But when he finally broke surface, our eyes could scarcely believe what they were seeing!"

"Go on, you brown-eyed mullet!" Tommy urged, smoking like a freight train in anticipation. "What happened then?"

George's huge, ruddy face was illuminated in firelight as he paused dramatically. When he continued, his voice was a shade lower and less boisterous in tone. "Ol Pervy was covered from helmet to boot in spiders. Bloody sea spiders the size of a fifty-cent piece."

Shona laid her book aside and leaned forward in her chair. At the same time, David turned from preparing the evening meal and stared at her.

"What?" she asked.

"Don't let that drunken ol' blitzer work you up with his bloody spider story," he told her, rolling his eyes.

"Aw, don't go on so!" Shona replied. "Now hush. I want to hear the rest of it."

At the neighboring campfire, the inebriated George continued his tale. "And they were unlike any spider I've ever seen in my life. At first, they appeared nearly *transparent*, as if made of glass. Then they would change colors... from aqua blue, to seaweed green, to coral pink. They clung to the diving suit like a babe latched to a Shelia's teat, refusing to let go. Andy Smith, the first mate, pulled up Pervy's air line and found that it had been *bitten through* and that the hollow of the hose was full of those bloody little web-spinners. We were afraid to bring poor ol' Pervy onboard, sure that the boat would be overrun by those blasted spiders, so we let him dangle in mid-air off portside. Andy pulled on a heavy pair of fishing gloves, leaned over, and swept the spiders off the face plate of the diving helmet. He unclasped the port door and we all had a look inside." George shuddered almost violently. "And do you know what we found? Inside that bloody diving suit we'd drug from the bottom of the Coral Sea?"

"Holy Dooley!" Just go on and tell 'im, George, you old ratbag!" snorted the third gentleman, shaking his head in disgust.

"Quit your knocking, Jimbo, and I'll do just that," George told him. He turned his eyes back to the young fellow. "Nothing but *bones*. Pervy White's bones. Those hellish sea spiders had gotten into his suit and stripped him of skin and sinew. All that remained was poor Pervy's eyes, as gray as shale, staring at us from the sockets of his skull, full of horror and regret!"

"Rubbish, pure and simple!" scoffed Jimbo. "Lying sack of shit!"

"No! It's all true!" George's face was dead serious in the flickering light of the campfire. "Those confounded sea spiders had done him in… eaten him alive. But he had reached the treasure he'd sought for so many years. For in his right glove was clutched a fistful of golden doubloons."

"So what did you blokes do then?" Tommy insisted on knowing.

"Just seeing what happened to ol' Pervy scared the remaining seven of us to our very core! Afraid to bring his carcass aboard, we… well, don't breathe a bloody word of this to *anyone*… but we cut 'im loose. Andy retrieved a pair of bolt cutters from the tool chest and snipped that cable, letting his boss and those devilish spiders drop into the sea, never to be seen again. When we returned to port, we told everyone that poor Pervy had been claimed by the ocean and was lost."

"And the gold?"

George turned his eyes toward Teewah Beach and the dark waters beyond. "Still out there, for all I know or care. The spiders have claimed it as their own booty. But they say if ever one comes upon the treasure and tries to steal it away, those sea spiders will come for it… and chew the bloody thief down to the bone for their treachery and vice."

The three at the campfire were silent for a long moment and then Jimbo began to laugh. "For that one, you deserve another grog, you old mongrel!" He tossed George another Powers, which the drunkard uncapped and chugged without hesitation, looking more than a little uncomfortable and introspective.

"Shona!" David said, his tone full of warning.

"What?"

"Please. No spider dreams tonight. I don't want you screaming bloody murder and scaring the girls and all of Cooloola out of their wits. Promise me?"

"Of course not!" she told him. "Do you actually think a silly old story like that would bother me?"

"Truthfully? Yes."

"Well, it won't. I'll sleep like a baby, you'll see."

But as David turned back to his dinner, he didn't seem quite so sure. And, to tell the truth, neither was Shona.

Shona found herself standing on the beach. Alone. In the dark.

Well, actually the darkness was not entirely whole. A full moon shone overhead, casting its pale glow upon the sand and reflecting on the rolling waves of the Coral Sea. Shona stood at the edge of the surf. The tide washed coolly across her bare feet, causing her to shudder. But, as she stood there

The Creeping Sands

by herself, she knew that her reaction had to do with something more than cold water.

She wore a pair of denim shorts and a navy windbreaker, but the clothing was heavy, uncomfortable. Shona turned her eyes toward the wooded stretch of the campground. She could barely see their camper in the dense shadows amid the trees. David and the girls slept peacefully inside. So why wasn't she there with them? Was she sleepwalking... or had something awakened her and drawn her to the water's edge?

Suddenly, she felt the sand shift beneath the soles of her feet. It was a movement that was nearly indiscernible at first. But then it continued, growing in speed and intensity. It wasn't her imagination. Something was underneath the sand of the beach; not just one thing, but many. She felt the loose grains roll like an earthen wave, heaving upward, throwing her off balance. Shona fell backward and landed on her bum on the beach.

When she hit, gleaming objects fell from the pockets of her jacket and shorts. Round and golden, they rolled across the sand, as though making their way back toward the sea.

"No!" her mind screamed. She scrambled on hands and knees, attempting to retrieve the doubloons. She felt an emotion well up within her, one that she was unaccustomed to. Greed. Seeing the golden coins roll away threw her into a wild panic. Her hands clutched frantically, grabbing up fistfuls of sand, shell, and gold. Hurriedly, she stuffed them back into her pockets.

A moment later, she realized her mistake. The sand beneath her surged once again and the surface broke, giving birth to the life that had burrowed, unseen, below. Spiders. All sizes and colors. Aqua blue. Coral pink. Algae green. The creatures crept from the depths of the beach, shrugging grains of sand from their backs and legs, tiny eyes gleaming at her accusingly in the moonlight.

"I... I'm sorry," she said, too late. "I'll put it back. I swear I will!"

But the sea spiders were not convinced. As she scrambled away in a crab-like scuttle, the spiders pursued her, not swiftly, but slowly and deliberately. Frightened, she looked toward the campground. The forest was darker and further away now. She could scarcely see the Landcruiser and its fold-out camper.

The golden coins jingled loudly in her pockets, drawing out more and more of the translucent spiders. They broke from the tight-packed confines of the sand, from beneath stone and shell. The multi-legged procession crept toward her at an even pace, unhurriedly, aware that escape was impossible. Shona tried to get to her feet, but each time the ground would shift beneath her, causing her to lose her balance.

Then as the spiders closed the gap, scrambling across her sand-caked toes and instep of her feet, Shona looked toward the ocean and was horrified to see a dark, seething wave rolling toward her. Not a wave of water, but of living, hungering spiders. She opened her mouth to scream, but before she could utter a single sound, the wave was upon her, burying her in its scrambling currents, filling her eyes and hair, her throat… choking, biting.

Her final thoughts were of David and Taylor and Hayley. Sleeping nearby, unsuspecting.

Snoozing peacefully… until voracious, flesh-consuming fury yanked them from their slumber, screaming…

Shona's eyes opened, staring frantically into the gloom above her. She thrust the fingers of her right hand into her mouth, biting down hard, stifling her own cry of alarm. *I will not scream! I refuse to wake everyone up and give David the satisfaction of being right about that damned spider story the old man old his mates!*

She closed her eyes and breathed deeply. As her teeth released her flesh, she tasted blood in her mouth. In the darkness, she could barely see the pale flesh of her hand and found that she had, indeed, broken the skin.

Why do these things torment you so? she demanded to know almost angrily. *Scarcely the size of your thumbnail and you act like they're rabid dingoes. Get a hold of yourself, girl! You're being bloody irrational!*

The Creeping Sands

Shona lay back down on the air mattress, running a hand through her dark hair. She was bathed in sweat, from head to toe, despite the coolness of the early summer evening. Next to her, David snored softly. A few feet away, on their own bed, her daughters slept motionlessly, not a care in the world.

What a dipstick you are, believing in such rubbish! she told herself. But before her nerves finally settled and she drifted back to sleep, she couldn't resist the impulse to stick her hands in the pockets of her shorts. The absence of coins—or anything else for that matter—should have eased her mind. But it didn't. Her thoughts were still occupied with lost treasure, devoured sea captains, and eight-legged creatures from the darkest depths of the ocean.

The following day was perfect. Bright and breezy with a cloudless sky and an ocean lazily lapping at the edge of Teewah and Rainbow Beaches, the latter called so because of the wide variety of colors its sand possessed.

Shona and David spent their morning relaxing, watching Taylor and Hayley play on the beach and do some boogie-boarding. The calm of the day helped alleviate some of the anxiety Shona had felt from the night before. The images of rampaging sea spiders seeking vengeance faded, banished by the girls' laughter and the sound of gulls overhead.

At noon, they returned to camp and had lunch; sandwiches and chips with their favorite soft drinks. While they ate, they watched with amusement as a four-wheel-drive—which had ventured too close to the surf—battled to release itself from the wet sand, digging its way deeper and deeper in the process. Taylor and Hayley looked at one another, aware that the driver's disaster was their gain. As soon as a wrecker hauled the vehicle onto firmer ground, the two girls left the remnants of their meal and headed for the deep ruts that the four-wheel-drive had left beneath its frantically churning tires.

Shona laughed as they ran toward the beach. She knew why they were so excited. Sometimes there were dozens of rare and beautiful shells buried deep in the sand, hidden from view. A man-made excavation such as a stuck vehicle could bring such treasures to the surface. Taylor and Hayley had been lucky before, widening the ruts with their hands and finding all kinds of neat stuff.

She was helping David clean up, when an excited shout drew their attention. Hayley was sprinting across the dunes to the campsite, her face ecstatic. Taylor, on the other hand, looked more than a little put-out, apparently for not making the discovery that her younger sister was so happy about.

"Look, Dad! Look, Mum!" Hayley shrilled, her eyes sparkling with triumph. "Look at what *I* found in the bottom of one of the tire tracks!"

"What is it, dear?' Shona asked her. She couldn't help but smile at her daughter's enthusiasm.

When the girl held the object into view, between her thumb and forefinger, Shona's heart fairly skipped a beat. For a second, she felt disoriented, almost on the verge of fainting.

Her daughter brandished a coin, but not just any form of currency. It was plainly gold and rather large in size. Despite its age, the markings were still discernable. It was foreign, clearly Spanish in origin.

"That's incredible, Hayley!" her father said, surprised. He took the coin and studied it carefully. "This has to be a doubloon. I'd stake my life on it! Come look at it, dear."

But Shona refused to step any closer. "Put it back."

David turned and looked at her as though she had sprouted a second head. "What?"

"I told her to put it back where she found it," Shona insisted.

Hayley's excitement faded and she began to pout. "Put it back? But why, Mum?"

"Because it's not yours. It belongs to someone else."

David regarded her, annoyed. "Shona, whoever this belonged to has been dead and gone for several hundred years. Finders Keepers, I say."

"Hurrah!" cheered Hayley. She snatched the coin from her father's fingers and danced around.

"Please, baby," Shona implored, feeling both frightened and angry with herself at the same time. "Just put it back. Or, better, toss it into the ocean. You know, like into a wishing well. Throw it as far as you can and make a wish."

"I'm not giving my money to the sea," Hayley said, stepping back a little.

Shona reached out and snatched at the coin. "Give it to me... *now!*"

David gently took his wife by the shoulders and turned her away from the children. "Shona, listen to yourself. You're sounding downright..."

"What?"

"Hysterical, that's what. I know what's going on. It's that story you overheard last night. The one that bloody drunk told his mates. That story about the spiders and the Spanish gold."

"No, that's not true." Shona could imagine how she looked at that moment: wild-eyed and scared out of her wits.

"Let's just drop it," David suggested in a low voice. "Let Hayley keep the coin. It's no big deal."

Of course it's no big deal, Shona told herself. Images of her beach dream resurfaced: the spiders erupting from the sand, the sea, pursuing her, covering her, in search of their precious treasure. *I certainly hope it's no big deal.*

"Can I, Mum?" Hayley asked her. "Can I keep it?"

Shona forced a smile. "Sure, baby. You can keep it."

"Cool!" Hayley flipped the corn and then stuck it in a pocket of her shorts.

"Good show," said David, kissing his wife on the cheek. "Let's clean up and we'll take a walk down the beach. Then later we'll build a fire and the girls can toast marshmallows."

Shona simply nodded, then followed him back to tidy up the lunch clutter. *Good show,* her husband had said… and he was right. For, although she didn't feel good about it at all, she intended to sneak the coin away from Hayley later that night and, when she got the chance, cast it back into the ocean where it belonged.

She awoke and stared into darkness.

At first, Shona was certain that she was reliving the nightmare of the spider attack in her bedroom. But then the familiar scents of canvas, dewy vegetation, and salt air came to her and she realized that she was at Cooloola and not home in Brisbane.

She breathed in deeply and let her eyes adjust to the gloom. Soon the faint glow of a half-moon shone from beyond the netted windows. She looked around her and saw the sleeping forms of her family: David on the big air mattress beside her and Taylor and Hayley on their own bed a few feet away. Shona felt for a flashlight they always carried on their camping trips and found it next to the mattress. She switched it on. Its pale circle of light illuminated the interior of the fold-out camper.

The Creeping Sands

Shona directed it toward Hayley. Her youngest daughter frowned and mumbled as the light engulfed her. Not wanting to wake her up, Shona clamped her palm partially over the beam, until only Hayley's right hand was revealed. Fisted in the child's palm was the gold doubloon, barely visible between her small fingers.

She considered trying to pry it loose, but knew there was little chance of doing that without waking her up. The Spanish coin was Hayley's pride and joy. Any effort to steal it away would produce one whale of a hissy-fit.

Shona switched off the flashlight and shifted uncomfortably on the air mattress. She would have felt a lot better if her original intention had gone according to plan. She could have sneaked out of the camper, down to the beach, and flung the coin into the dark waters of the Coral Sea. Then maybe she would have had a little peace of mind. But Hayley's pride in her prize and her tenacity at keeping it close at hand had foiled Shona's best efforts at attempting to gain possession of it. Just knowing that it was in the camper with them somehow filled her with an underlying dread that was difficult to explain. It was almost a guilty sensation, as though they had stolen something precious from someone and the owner was currently in search of it.

Get that bloody wives' tale out of your head, Shona! she scolded herself. *It was just a bunch of bluff and bellow, that's all.*

Shona leaned on one elbow and, just out of curiosity, pulled back the canvas flap of the camper window and looked through the mesh screen. The beach looked tranquil in the moonlight. The sands were pale and unblemished, while the whitecaps of the waves rolled gently inland.

She sighed. *Just relax and try to get some sleep.*

Shona was about to turn away from the window, when something odd caught her attention.

The beach was *moving*. Not the tide washing across the sand, but the beach itself. The pale surface had seemed to split open in several places and swaths of dark shadow was seeping up from its depths, broadening, growing larger with each passing moment.

Shona's heart began to pound. She reached over and gently shook her husband. "David!" she whispered. "David… wake up!"

David groaned and rolled over. "Hmmm? What's wrong?"

"Look at this."

"At *what*?" She could hear the irritation in his voice.

"Just look out the window and tell me if you see what I see."

David sat up in bed turned and peered through the screen. After a moment, Shona could sense him stiffen in alarm. "What the hell is that?"

She joined him at the window. A large portion of Teewah Beach was obscured by the thickening shadow now. They watched as the pool of blackness suddenly shifted direction and headed across the dunes… straight for their campsite.

"Oh God… they're coming for us!"

"Who?" asked David. "You're not talking about those bloody…"

"Spiders? Yes, that's exactly what I'm talking about. And they're on their way. Just look at them!"

As the swath of darkness grew nearer, they could see that it was not a single entity that moved toward them, but thousands, perhaps millions of living things, traveling en masse. From a distance they almost appeared to be tiny, black crabs… but they weren't. They were spiders, skittering their way across the sand and sawgrass, toward Cooloola Campground.

David sat up, clearly concerned. "Damn! They *are* coming this way!"

Shona thought about the camper and a dozen tiny gaps in the canvas walls where something as small as a spider would be able to enter without any trouble at all. Her thoughts went back to

George the Drunkard's story about the sea captain's remains, trapped within the diving suit, stripped clean of flesh.

"We need to get out of here... *now*!" she told him.

"But where...?"

"The Toyota. We'll lock ourselves in there and they won't be able to get to us."

She could hear David pulling on his sneakers in the dark. "It's worth a try. But we better hurry. They may get here before we can reach it."

Shona knew he was right. The multitude of spiders was closing the ground between the sea and the camper swiftly, almost with an urgency that was human in nature. Or maybe it was hunger and vengeance that drove them. A disturbing image came to mind; an image of her rolling on the ground, covered in hundreds of ravenous spiders—screaming and flailing—as she heard the terrified cries of the rest of her family splitting the night air only a few feet away.

She got up and went to the girls' bed. "Taylor. Taylor, honey, wake up."

"Leave me alone," her eldest daughter moaned, rolling over.

"Baby, we've got to go. We've got to get to the Toyota."

Taylor sat up groggily. "Why? Is there a storm coming?"

"Yes," Shona told her truthfully. "A very bad one. Now come on."

On the opposite side of the air mattress, David was trying to wake up Hayley, with no luck. The youngster was the type that could have slept through a hurricane, especially after a long day of playing on the beach. "She's not budging."

"Just carry her." Shona slipped her feet into her own sneakers and, as an afterthought, stuck the flashlight into the waistband of her sleep shorts. Then helping Taylor to her feet, she started toward the camper door.

They unfastened the flap and were shocked to see the dark pool of creeping blackness cresting the dunes, only a short distance away. As they stepped out into the open, they could hear a brittle skittering as millions of tiny legs moved in tandem, saturating the ground until no sign of earth could be seen underneath.

"Run!" yelled David. Together, each toting a child, they crossed the short distance between camper and vehicle.

The doors will be locked, Shona told herself. *We won't be able to get in!* But when she got there, the handle gave no resistance and the door opened easily. She dumped Taylor into the back seat at the same instant her husband placed Hayley inside. Then, slamming the rear doors shut, both of them pulled open the driver's and passenger's doors. It was at that moment that the ground around them grew dark and busy. The two hopped in and closed the doors securely behind them. Instinctively, Shona locked her side.

"What? Are they going to bloody lift the handle up?" David asked her.

"Who knows *what* they can do?" Shona snapped. "If they can erupt out of the sand and pour out of the ocean, they're not like regular spiders, now are they?"

David grew quiet and said nothing.

They waited, but heard nothing. Then they detected a sound almost like the random pattering of raindrops on the metal panels of the four-wheel-drive. It took a moment before they realized what the noise really was. It was the sound of spiders leaping forcefully onto the sides and fenders of the vehicle.

"What are you waiting for?" Shona asked him. "Start it up and let's go!"

David stared at her. "Have you forgotten something? The camper is still on the hitch. With it all folded out, there's no way we can get through the trees to the main road. We'll get wedged in for sure."

She knew he was right. All they could do was sit there and wait. But wait for *what*?

"Shona, I'm going to turn on the headlights."

"No… please. Just leave it dark."

"I have to know what the hell we're dealing with." Then, without hesitation, he flipped on the lights.

Their worst fears were suddenly revealed, naked and unconcealed by shadow and gloom. Thousands of spiders, similarly shaped, but of varied sizes, were scrambling across the dunes, skittering across the fenders and hood of the Toyota, and even dangling from the foliage of the black casuarina trees overhead.

"Mum!" Taylor's voice changed from sleepy to shrill with panic in a split second. "Mum, are those…?"

"Turn it off!" Shona yelled. "Now!"

"You don't have to tell me twice!" David's hand trembled as he extinguished the headlights.

Sitting in the darkness, they heard the *skritch-skritch-skritch* of the arachnids crawling across the steel body of the Landcruiser. Frantically, they washed across the hood and up the windshield. The vehicle lurched as the weight of the invaders increased, bearing down on the shocks.

Shona watched, horrified, as spiders coated the glass of the windshield, blocking out all nocturnal light. She wasn't sure why, but she reached out and laid the flat of her palm against the inner glass. Almost instantly, they changed color, transforming from black to gray to the same hue as her olive complexion. She recalled what George had said; how the sea spiders held the colors of seaweed, coral, and sea. It appeared as though they were almost chameleon in nature.

"Camper or no camper, I'm getting us out of here," David said.

He turned the key in the ignition, but the engine struggled, unable to crank into life. The belt pulleys ground and squealed as though obstructed. Shona could imagine thousands of spiders beneath the hood, gumming the works, using their bodies to prevent their escape.

Suddenly, the windshield popped and a long, silver crack appeared horizontally from left to right. The weight of the spiders was growing too great for the glass to withstand.

"Daddy!" squealed Taylor from the back seat.

"Shut your eyes, luv!" he called. There was a mounting hopelessness in his voice that Shona had never heard before.

Then it came to her. She leapt out of her seat and reached into the back, feeling for Hayley in the darkness. She found her shoulder and then felt her way down her right arm to her tightly-clasped hand. Shona gently pried at her fingers, attempting to work them loose from the object she held.

"No," mumbled her daughter, pouting in her sleep. "No, it's mine."

"Let me have it, baby," Shona said soothingly. "I'm just going to polish it... make it all bright and pretty for you."

A smile crossed her freckled face. "Alright, Mum." Then she let loose and Shona had the doubloon in her possession.

"Are you serious?" asked David when he saw the coin.

"Do you have any better ideas?"

"No," admitted her husband. "I suppose not."

The windshield cracked again, this time diagonally. The safety glass began to bow slowly inward. If it gave away completely, the interior of the Land Cruiser would be full of the angry spiders in only a matter of seconds.

Shona laid her hand on the window handle on the passenger door.

"You're not actually going to..."

"I have to," Shona told her husband.

She worked the handle a fraction of an inch and shoved the doubloon into the tiny crack at the top of the window. Almost

The Creeping Sands

immediately, a spider—much larger than the others—was there. Its incisors, wickedly curved and coated with venom, took hold of the coin in a vise-like grip that literally yanked it from her grasp. She watched as the coin disappeared. Quickly, she rolled the window back up tightly.

They waited a long, breathless moment. Then the windshield stopped settling and the body of the Toyota slowly returned to its original position as the weight of the sea spiders began to lessen, little by little. Soon, they could see through the windshield, which had been on the verge of collapse a second ago. The dark wave was retreating, returning to the beach.

Shona opened her door.

"No!" David reached out and grabbed her arm.

"It's okay. I think they got what they came for."

She stepped out of the Toyota and stood on the lower jamb of the open door, elevating herself so that she could see better. The swarm of spiders was across the sand now and merging with the dark currents of the Coral Sea.

It wasn't long before they were gone entirely, as though they had never been there at all.

The drive home was unnervingly quiet.

Shona, David, and Taylor said little to one another on the way back to Brisbane. Only Hayley—who had slept through the entire ordeal—was peppy and energetic.

Shona had expected her to be upset over the disappearance of her coin, but strangely enough it hadn't seemed to have bothered her all that much. Something else occupied her mind. Hayley kept telling everyone that she had a secret. One that she wouldn't reveal until they got home.

When they arrived, Shona and the girls started carrying their camping supplies inside, while David simply stood there and shook his head, appraising the damage to the Landcruiser. The windshield was cracked in a dozen places and the Toyota's body was dimpled from the weight of the spiders, looking as though it had been through one nasty hailstorm. They hadn't expected to get the four-wheel-drive started, but eventually they had. Upon checking the engine, they found only gummy strands of webbing amid the hoses and belt pulleys. Otherwise, there hadn't been a single sign of a spider having been there.

They ate a light dinner and then Shona helped the girls get ready for bed. Taylor was asleep a minute after she climbed beneath the covers, but Hayley was still exuberant. She sat cross-legged in bed with an almost mischievous grin on her face.

"Don't you want to know?" she asked.

"Know what?" Shona plumped Hayley's pillow for her and laid it at the head of the bed.

"My secret." The eight-year-old continued to smile that peculiar smile, her eyes twinkling.

"Oh, right." Shona turned on the faint glow of the nightstand lamp. Wearily, she sat on the edge of the bed. "Okay, go ahead. What's your big secret?"

Hayley seemed scarcely able to contain her excitement. "You know that gold coin I found in the sand? That doubloon?"

Shona sighed. She didn't even want to think about that awful coin and the trouble it had brought them. "Yeah, I know. What about it?"

Hayley reached up behind her mother's right ear, as though she were performing a particularly clever magic trick. As her hand retreated, Shona caught a glimpse of sparkling gold and her heart froze in her chest.

The Creeping Sands

"Well, I didn't find just one," Hayley told her proudly. "I found *two*."

Instantly, the room dimmed as the moonlight from outside was blocked from view. Shona didn't turn toward the window, for she knew what was there.

A wave of darkness, obscuring the glass panes and spreading quickly, like the creeping sands of Teewah Beach.

Hugs and Kisses

Tabby met Chad online.

It was a phone app called Lonesome Teen. Not a dating app really... just a place for awkward kids her age to meet and hang out. Trade photos, talk about hobbies and interests, sort of feel like you were wanted and accepted. Overall, it was pretty innocent. Nerds and goths mostly, sometimes more extreme outcasts; Emo, the heavy metal /death metal crowd, and weirdos who lived and breathed horror movies. Every now and then, a troublemaker or perv would show up.

Once, a boy from New Jersey sent Tabby a dick pic. The poor little thing had looked so sad and shriveled that she had giggled almost non-stop for three days. She had almost gotten into trouble in Mr. Blanchard's third-period algebra class, thinking of that itty-bitty penis, all nestled in a warm nest of downy pubic hair. She had snorted through her nose and laughed out loud, until the teacher had sternly threatened her with detention. Tabby was certain that he would lighten up and laugh, too, if she showed him the photo... but also knew it would violate the school's Zero-Tolerance policy and create a great scandal at George Wallace Central High, one that would grieve her mom and dad to no end, so she wisely kept it to herself.

Hugs and Kisses

Then came Chad. He had just contacted her out of nowhere; probably seen her profile and made some sort of connection with her photo. He wasn't brash or bragging like some of the boys she had encountered on LT. No, he was sweet and polite, and really seemed curious about her. Things started out slowly at first. You know, the "getting-to-know-one-another" period.

HI.

HI BACK. MY NAME IS TABBY.

TABBY... AS IN TABITHA? LIKE THAT LITTLE GIRL ON BEWITCHED... OR STEPHEN KING'S WIFE?

She didn't understand either reference, so she simply said YES... I GUESS SO.

I'M CHAD. YOUR INFO SAYS YOU ARE FROM ALABAMA.

YES... MONTGOMERY. HOW ABOUT YOU?

OH, HERE AND THERE. I TRAVEL A LOT. YOUR PHOTO LOOKS NICE.

Chad's photo was a little unfocused and blurry. A pale boy with huge blue eyes and no hair. Did he have leukemia or something?

YOU'RE CUTE, CHAD.

....

Had she scared him off?

CHAD?

I'M NOT CUTE... NOT REALLY. KIND OF AWKWARD. ALL ARMS AND LEGS.

SAME HERE. I'M... SORT OF OVERWEIGHT... TOO MUCH ACNE. WEAR GLASSES. NO GREAT BEAUTY.

YOU'RE BEAUTIFUL TO ME.

Tabby's heart had somersaulted in her chest. No boy had ever... EVER... said anything to her like that before.

AWWWW... THANKS!

Thus began their mutual friendship. And, before long, something much more.

It started with simple stuff, like their interests. Tabby liked Japanese anime, cosplay (but only in the privacy of her own bedroom), collecting Funko Pops, and watching Tik-Tok videos. Chad enjoyed reading (old stuff like Tolkien, Bradbury, and HG Wells), playing video games (Halo, Fallout, Mortal Kombat), and listening to country music (she forgave him for that.) She talked about her family; Mom, Dad, her big sister, Heather, the snotty cheerleader, their goldendoodle, Mister Fluffy. Chad skirted the issue for a while, then admitted that he was an orphan. He reluctantly admitted that his mother and father had abandoned him...didn't want to have anything to do with him at all... after he was born.

I LIVE WITH AN UNCLE, SORT OF. HE RUNS A TRAVELING CARNIVAL. I HELP OUT SOMETIMES.

THAT SOUNDS INTERESTING.

YEAH... IT IS. SOMETIMES TOO INTERESTING.

Then, she had asked him. The thing that had been on her mind after seeing his profile photo.

ARE... ARE YOU... UH... SICK?

SICK? OH, THAT. NO HAIR. LOL! I WAS BORN THAT WAY... IT'S A CONDITION. FAULTY GENES OR SOMETHING.

I'M SORRY. I DIDN'T MEAN TO HURT YOUR FEELINGS.

A pause. Then... YOU COULD NEVER DO THAT, TABBY. I... I LO... LIKE YOU. A LOT.

Again, cardiac gymnastics. Had he almost said that he *loved* her?

I LIKE YOU, TOO. She took the plunge.. the commitment. MORE THAN LIKE.

Another pause. Followed by...

Hugs and Kisses

XOXOXO!

Hugs and kisses.

And, just like that, they were boyfriend and girlfriend. An odd and alien concept in Tabby's isolated thoughts, but one that made her feel... almost... normal.

A month later, Tabby was walking down the hallway to biology class, when she saw a flyer tacked to the school bulletin board. It read McGREGOR'S CARNIVAL! THRILLS, CHILLS, EXCITEMENT! RIDES AND CONCESSIONS GALORE! DEMOLISION DERBY AND FREAK SHOW... FREE WITH ADMISSION!

The girl had felt a queasy sensation in her stomach. McGregor? Wasn't that Chad's uncle's name?

During the ride home on the school bus, she had pulled up the app and texted.

THERE'S A CARNAVAL COMING TO TOWN NEXT WEEK. McGREGOR'S. ISN'T THAT YOUR UNCLE?

A pause. Then... UH, YEAH.

SO, YOU'LL BE THERE?

Another pause. Long and tedious. Like sitting in the drive-thru at McDonald's at lunchtime.

YES. BUT... YOU SHOULDN'T COME.

She felt hurt. BUT I WANT TO MEET YOU.

YOU... JUST SHOULDN'T. LET'S LEAVE EVERYTHING THE WAY IT IS NOW. PLEASE?

She felt like she wanted to tear up. BUT, I THOUGHT YOU... LOVED ME. She included six crying emoji faces for emphasis.

I... DO. REALLY, MORE THAN ANYTHING. I JUST DON'T WANT TO... SCARE YOU.

WHY WOULD YOU DO THAT? SCARE ME?

I'M NOT NORMAL, TABBY. THE NO-HAIR THING... IT'S NOT THE ONLY THING. MY CONDITION... THERE'S MORE TO IT.

I DON'T CARE. I WANT TO SEE YOU. IT MIGHT BE OUR ONLY CHANCE.

Another pause. Lengthy and introspective on his part. She sensed that, despite his misgivings, he wanted to see her, too.

OKAY. I'LL BE IN THE LAST TENT ON THE LEFT. BUT YOU GOTTA PROMISE.

SURE. ANYTHING... ANYTHING AT ALL.

YOU CAN'T SCREAM OR CRY OR FAINT. PLEASE... PROMISE ME THAT.

Something about that chain of reactions tied Tabby's stomach into knots.

OKAY... I PROMISE.

And then it was settled. The following Friday night. Their first meeting, face to face. Around eight o'clock.

Their first, official date, so to speak.

It seemed like an eternity before Friday night rolled around.

Tabby had gotten permission from her parents to go, saying that she would tag along with some friends at school. Which was a lie, since no one at school really wanted to have anything to do with her. Luckily, the carnival was only a half mile from her house, so she walked there. She paid for her admission with money she had made babysitting.

The carnival was small and sort of rundown. Not like the county fair at all. The rides were old and showed signs of rust, and the midway booths held games and prizes that were outdated and uninteresting. The greasy aromas of foot-long corndogs, funnel cakes, and deep-fried Twinkies from the concession trailers would have normally enticed her, but she had no appetite that night. She felt oddly sick at her stomach, more out of fear and nervousness than anything else.

When she reached the end of the midway, she regarded the big white tent that had been pitched to the left. The banner that hung over the flap of the doorway confused her. *This can't be the right one,* she thought to herself. *What would he be doing in there?*

The banner read: BE AMAZED & HORRIFIED! FREAKS & HUMAN ODDITIES! THE SKELETON WOMAN! LITTLE PADDY, THE LEPRAUCHAN! THE TARANTULA BOY! THE MAN OF A MILLION TATTOOS!

Tabby stood at the doorway, hesitant to enter. *Maybe he's like a sideshow barker or something.* Then, taking a deep breath, she went inside.

The interior of the tent was gloomy, with the only illumination coming from spotlights hanging above each partitioned booth. The first one was Little Paddy, which was no more than a dwarf dressed up in the green garb of a leprechaun. He sat atop an iron kettle of faux gold coins, looking bored and restless... and like he might cuss you out if you stared at him long enough. The next was the Skeleton Woman. She was tall and so skinny that the bones of her pelvis and ribcage stood out in sharp relief. Tabby thought she looked a lot like an anorexic Meth addict than anything. The third was the tattooed man. He was broad and muscular and every inch of his body seemed to be etched with elaborate artwork. As she walked past, he stuck out his tongue, displaying an uncanny portrait of Elvis Presley tattooed on his taste buds. Tabby cringed at that and hurriedly moved on.

When she reached the final booth in the tent, she stopped, frozen, and stared. The thing that occupied the booth stared back... just as shocked and unnerved as she was.

It was a boy. Pale to the point of being snow white, completely hairless, with six arms and two legs. His eyes—sky blue in color—

were huge in the shadowy pits of their sockets… three times larger than normal eyes. His teeth were yellowed, crooked, and sharp at the tips. The only article of clothing he wore was a pair of boxer shorts, bright red in color with gold stripes down the sides. He perched on what looked like a massive cobweb. Not a fake one made of ropes or wires, or even industrial-strength Halloween cobwebs. No, it looked real. The silky strands must have been strong to have held the weight of the thing that clung to it.

Tabby looked into that face. It was a face she had grown to love, to regard as handsome and compassionate. The face of her soulmate… but in stark detail, not blurry and unfocused like the photograph.

"Hi, Tabby," he said. The expression on his face was sad and apologetic.

The girl tried to speak… tried to form words several times… before it finally came out. "Chad?"

"Yes. It's me." The Tarantula Boy swayed slightly on his web. "It's nice to finally meet you."

Tabby shook her head, as if trying to clear her thoughts. "What… what are you doing… dressed up like *that*?"

Chad's pale face reddened in embarrassment. "All this… it's for real. It's me. The way I am."

She tried her best to stop it, but tears bloomed in her eyes. "Oh, Chad…"

The boy could sense her disappointment and confusion. "I'm sorry. I tried to warn you. You… shouldn't have come."

"Yes," she said with a sob. "You're right. I shouldn't have."

Chad began to crawl down the huge web toward her, while she backed away in horror. "Please, Tabby… sweetheart… don't."

The girl's heart pounded in her chest, almost painfully so. "I'm sorry, but… I can't." Then she turned and ran for the open flap of the tent.

"I'm sorry," his voice echoed behind her. "Really sorry."

Hugs and Kisses

Squalling like a baby, she ran past the other spectators in the tent, wanting nothing more than to get out of there and go home.

The last thing she heard him say before she reached the noise and commotion of the midway was "I still love you, Tabby!"

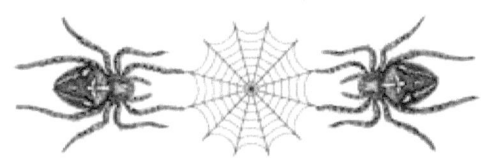

Her phone dinged around eleven-thirty.

Tabby had laid on her bed in the darkness since returning home. All cried out, feeling sad... feeling lost. The sound of the text caused her heart to skip a beat. Frantically, she scrambled across the mattress and grabbed her phone off the nightstand. She slipped on her glasses so that she could see better.

TABBY?

She stared at her name as if it belonged to someone else. It was like she didn't even know herself anymore.

TABBY... ARE YOU OKAY?

Tabby felt like she wanted to cry again, but for a different reason. CHAD! OH, I'M SO SORRY. I SHOULDN'T HAVE ACTED THAT WAY. I'M SO ASHAMED!!

DON'T BE. PLEASE... I EXPECTED IT. IT WAS UNDERSTANDABLE ... HOW YOU REACTED.

BUT IT WAS SO WRONG!! I'M SORRY, BABY!

I LOVE YOU, TABBY.

Her fingers couldn't type fast enough. I LOVE YOU, TOO. SO MUCH!

There was a pause of fifteen seconds or more. TABBY... I'VE RUN AWAY.

WHAT DO YOU MEAN?

FROM THE CARNIVAL. MR. McGREGOR... HE'S MEAN. DOESN'T TREAT ME WELL. FEEDS ME SCRAPS FROM THE CONCESSION STANDS. HITS ME SOMETIMES. IT'S WORSE THAN BEING THE ELEPHANT MAN!

Tabby's heart sank. The thought of someone hurting him was devastating.

IT WAS TIME FOR ME TO GO. I SLIPPED AWAY...BEFORE HE COULD LOCK ME IN MY CAGE.

A CAGE? OH, CHAD! Her mind raced. WHERE ARE YOU NOW?

I'M AT A PARK... A COUPLE OF BLOCKS FROM THE CARNIVAL.

I KNOW WHERE IT IS. I'M COMING!

I DON'T WANT YOU TO GET IN TROUBLE WITH YOUR PARENTS...

I'M COMING! THAT'S ALL THERE IS TO IT!

Tabby grabbed a sweater off her bedpost and quietly made her way down the upstairs hallway, past the bedroom where her parents slept, and her sister's room. She could hear Heather on the other side of the door, laughing and indulging in a group chat with her friends.

When she finally reached the back door and let herself out, she sighed in relief, then headed down the empty street of the subdivision, toward the park.

She found him sitting on the top bleachers of the softball field. He was hunched over, wearing a red and gold silk robe with six sleeves instead of two. On the back was embroidered THE TERRIFYING TARANTULA BOY!

Tabby mounted the bleacher stairs, feeling a little winded when she finally reached the top. Chad stood up and they stared at one another for a long, tense moment. He smiled in an endearing way that hid his jagged, yellow teeth and threw his six arms wide. Without hesitation she ran into them and held him tightly.

Hugs and Kisses

They sat down and remained like that for a long time. Hugging, kissing, just glad to be together after only experiencing each other in bold text on narrow smartphone screens for so long. There was no furious fondling of teenage lust, no loss of control. Their relationship went beyond such immature trivialities. They were in love and, at that moment, that was all that they needed.

After a while, they simply sat and held one another, nestled inside the red silk carnival robe.

"Tell me," she whispered. "Tell me about you... about your life."

Chad hesitated and then nodded.

He told her of his estranged parents. How his mother discovered that she suffered from cancer when she was pregnant with him and how her options for survival had dwindled in the days following her diagnosis. In desperation, she and his father had traveled to South America for an experimental treatment. It had stopped the cancer, but did something terrible to their unborn son. It was said that she screamed wildly and had to be sedated when she saw Chad for the first time. He was never held... never loved... by his biological parents. He guessed it took a special degree of compassion and courage to raise a child with six arms.

But, someone had. A middle-aged couple in Minnesota... foster parents who loved and nurtured children like him. The house where he grew up was full of them; children without arms or legs, some with too many, some with no mouths or ears or eyes, others with a triple portion that made them look more like cartoon characters than human beings. They were so happy there, able to be themselves without shame or ridicule, loved unconditionally by those two sweet souls.

Then, one Saturday morning, the man and woman left on a trip to the grocery store and never came back. They were killed instantly in a head-on collision with a dump truck. The family Chad had known most of his life suddenly fell apart. Child Services broke them up, placed them in homes all over the state. Homes that wanted that government aid check every month, but not them. Chad had moved from one home to another, finally ending up at Sam and Betty McGregor's. Betty had tried her best to care for him and offer him a better life. She thought Chad could do anything he wanted, be anything that he dreamt of being. Sam McGregor, on the other hand, had other ideas. He wanted to exploit the little "spider boy", feature him in his traveling carnival. Betty would hear nothing of it. With her around, Chad had a chance for a normal life, maybe college after high school and opportunities beyond his infirmities. When Betty died of pneumonia the winter of Chad's thirteenth birthday, those hopes and dreams died. He had no choice and became a permanent star in McGregor's degrading sideshow. The only thing the man let the boy keep from his former life was his cell phone. It was his only link between his dismal existence and the outside world.

His only link to something good and decent... to someone like *her*.

"I'm sorry," Tabby said, nestling closer. "That life has been so hard for you."

Chad sighed. "Sometimes I wonder why God made me this way... if it wasn't for a good reason."

"Maybe it is," she told him hopefully. "Maybe you just haven't found it yet."

They sat there quietly for a while. The digital sign of the bank across the street revealed the time as a little past two in the morning. A question came to mind... one Tabby hesitated to ask.

"That web in the side show... did McGregor make it or did—?"

"I have a gland," said Chad. "On my lower back, just above my butt. It's sort of disgusting." He couldn't help but laugh. "It does make me feel like Spiderman sometimes, though."

Tabby embraced him. Multiple arms held her securely.

Hugs and Kisses

"Come home with me, Chad," she told him without a second thought. "No one ever goes into our attic. You can live there as long as you want. Even if my parents discovered you, it would be okay. They're good people. They would learn to love you... like I do."

Chad's expression darkened. "No, they wouldn't. People only see what's in front of them... in the flesh. They can't see past the extra arms... the buggy eyes... the crooked fangs. They can't see past the monster... the freak. The poor, deformed Tarantula Boy. Mrs. Betty was the only one... and you."

"What will you do?" she asked, frightened. "Where will you go?"

Chad looked around the dark expanse of the park. His eyes settled on a thick stretch of forest with a tranquil walking trail and a peaceful stream running through it. "There. I'll make my home in the trees. I'm a great climber and I can build my own treehouse. I don't get hot in the summer or cold in the winter like you do; I have a way to regulate my temperature. And I can hunt and catch my own food. Birds and squirrels... fish from the creek. It's sure better than cold hotdogs and stale popcorn."

"But you can't live in the wild," she protested. "It's not right."

"More right than wrong," he told her. "At least, that's how I feel."

There was a dozen reasons Tabby wanted to give for why he shouldn't do it. *What if you're discovered? What if a jogger or some kids see you and call the police? What if you're captured and they take you back to the carnival... or, worse, the zoo? What if you trend on Twitter or go viral on YouTube? What if you really, truly become the Terrifying Tarantula Boy?*

But she kept quiet and voiced none of them.

As the pale glow of sunrise peeked over the trees from the east, they parted. They descended the bleachers. Tabby turned toward the direction of home, Chad toward the dense stretch of woods. Before they went their separate ways, they kissed and cried.

"Will I ever see you again?" she asked.

"Maybe," he said. "Maybe not. Maybe it's better if we just remember this night and how special it was."

She nodded. Tabby removed her glasses and wiped her eyes with the sleeve of her sweater. "I love you, Chad."

"Love you, too. Don't forget me."

Tabby's heart ached. "Never."

She stood and watched as he walked into the woods and stopped beneath a towering oak tree. He smiled and waved, then bent down and, in a weird way, sort of like standing on his head. A silky, white rope shot upward into the branches and, a moment later, he went with it.

Tabby almost laughed and cried at the same time. It would have been hysterically comical, if it hadn't been so very tragic.

Twelve years passed.

It was a bright, sunny day in the spring of the year. Tabby and her children—a son and daughter—walked the wooded walking trail, laughing and enjoying the April breeze and the sound of songbirds in the tall trees.

"We're going ahead, Mom," said Kathy. "To the bridge over the creek."

"Be careful," she told them. "David… hold your sister's hand. And don't lean over the railing and fall in!"

Soon, they had run around a bend in the pathway and were out of sight.

Tabby paused beneath a big oak and breathed deeply. Her thoughts often turned inward during her forays into the forest by the park. Things had turned out well for her since those awkward, lonesome teenage days. She had a wonderful family… a wonderful life. The glasses and acne were long gone. She still sported a few extra pounds, but that was okay. That was who she was and she was comfortable with that fact.

She was about to follow her kids, when she heard a voice.

"Tabby."

It came from above her.

Her heart beat faster. "Chad?"

"Close your eyes, Tabby, and keep them closed." A man's deep voice, full of confidence and power. Nothing like the shy, halting tones of adolescence.

"Okay," she replied and waited.

A rustle of leaves sounded from the branches above her and, suddenly, arms embraced her, strongly, but tenderly. She felt her feet leave the ground for a moment and, at first, thought she would go soaring through the treetops, maybe even beyond, to the sky. The thought both frightened and exhilarated the woman.

Then, a second later, she felt the soles of her sneakers touch the pavement of the walking trail once again.

"That was…nice," she whispered.

"Yes… wasn't it?"

She cracked her eyelids a bit, caught a blur of a strong, handsome face and bright blue eyes between the veil of her lashes.

"No cheating now," he reprimanded. "You promised. Eyes closed."

She nodded, then felt soft lips against her own. Tabby didn't regard it as cheating on her husband. It was more like a simple, affectionate kiss between two old friends.

She felt his arms leave her and experienced a longing… one that had never quite gone away. When his voice came again, it was distant, far above her.

"I left you a message at home."

She waited a long moment, then opened her eyes. When she looked up into the uppermost reaches of the oak, all she saw were heavy, gnarled branches and the green brilliance of new leaves.

When they were done at the park, Tabby and the kids stopped for ice cream, then went home. She saw what he had left almost immediately, carved in a wooden support of the back deck.

XOXOXO

And the smile that it brought lasted until nightfall... then returned, afresh, early the next morning.

Come See Spider Cave!

They were thirty-five miles from Chattanooga, when something caught Joe Stanton's attention.

"No way!" he said, smiling. "I can't believe it."

His wife, Cindy, glanced up from the Amish romance novel she had been reading. "Can't believe what?"

Brandon and Lacey craned their necks from the back seat. "What is it, Dad?"

Joe could barely contain his excitement. *"That!"*

It was a billboard; pretty weathered, maybe twenty feet by thirty. They had seen others during their trip—SEE ROCK CITY! and EXPLORE RUBY FALLS!—but this one was different. It was wreathed with monstrous depictions of spiders. Tarantulas, black widows, brown recluse. Legs splayed menacingly, eyes twinkling with malice, mandibles gnashing hungrily.

The sign read: COME SEE SPIDER CAVE! LARGEST UNDERGROUND ARACHNID SANCTUARY IN THE SOUTHERN UNITED STATES! THRILLS & CHILLS! SOUVENIRS & SNACK BAR! TAKE EXIT 224 AND TURN RIGHT. DRIVE 12 MILES AND YOU'RE THERE!

"Wow," said Joe. "My folks used to take me there when I was a kid. I haven't thought of that place in years."

His daughter wrinkled her nose in disgust. "Spiders. Yuck!"

Cindy nodded. "I agree. Double yuck! Drive on."

Exit 224 was fast approaching and the car began to slow as Joe tapped the mini-van's brakes. "Come on, guys! Let's be adventurous. Spider Cave awaits!"

"Let's go, Dad!" Brandon reached over and skittered his fingers across his sister's bare arm, eliciting a squeal. "Let's explore the spiders' subterranean lair!" He leered sinisterly in Lacey's direction. "Bwahahaha!"

"Mom! Make Brandon quit!"

"Stop tormenting your sister, Brand." Cindy turned to Joe. "I think we just need to go on to Lookout Mountain and forget this little detour. You know I'm not a big fan of creepy-crawlers, especially spiders."

But, abruptly, Exit 224 was there and the van was veering off the interstate and tooling down the ramp. "Oh... I'm sorry, dear. I thought we decided to..."

Cindy shook her head, admitting defeat. "Okay! Just go! If it means that much to you, we'll endure it. Not that my opinion is worth considering..."

Lacey laughed. "Awww... you're going to be in the doghouse, Dad!"

"No," said her pesky brother. Brandon reached over and ran jittery fingers through his sister's blond hair. "He's going to be in the Spider Cave... and so are we!"

"MOM!"

Cindy sighed and returned her attention to puritan passions in idyllic Pennsylvania. "Y'all hush and let me read in peace, will you?"

Come See Spider Cave!

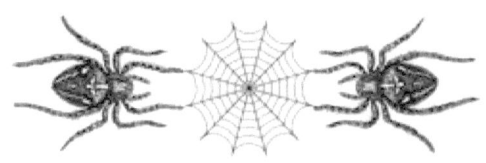

When they finally got there, it wasn't at all like Joe remembered it to be. Just a long building that resembled a convenience store nestled against the rocky base of a wooded hill. Faded wooden signs proclaimed SPIDERS! SPIDERS! AND EVEN MORE SPIDERS!, THRILLING & EDUCATIONAL TOURS HOURLY!, and PLUNGE 1,000 FEET TO THE CORE OF THE EARTH!

Cindy marked her book and left it on the dash of the Caravan. "Looks like a dump to me. You sure it's still in business?'

Joe scratched his head and looked around. "Well… I think so." There was only one occupant in the row of guest parking spaces out front; a Ford dually pickup hauling a twenty-two-foot, silver Airstream camper. The only other vehicle that could be seen was a Chevy Bronco parked to the right of the building, where an ice machine stood on the far corner. The man seemed disappointed. "It sure looks smaller than I remember."

"What about this big plunge?" asked Lacey. "I'm not a straight-A student in science, Dad, but I think there's more than a thousand feet till you reach the center of the Earth."

"One thousand, eight hundred, and two miles, to be exact," Brandon, who *was* a straight A student, told her. "It's just a marketing gimmick… right, Dad? To hook the crowds and get them in the door."

His mom smirked and looked around. "Oh, right. The crowds are swarming for miles."

"It's an elevator," Joe explained. "You know, like at Ruby Falls. It takes you a thousand feet down to the cavern."

Cindy still wasn't impressed. "An elevator? This place? I'm surprised they have a working toilet."

"Come on, dear… you're spoiling my boyish enthusiasm."

His wife laughed, hugged him around the waist, and gave him a peck on the cheek. "Aw, poor baby. Am I bursting your spider-loving bubble?"

Brandon almost said *Get a room, you two*, but caught himself before he did. The twelve-year-old didn't want to upset his mother and ruin his chance of seeing the Largest Arachnid Sanctuary in the Southern United States.

Joe grinned as Cindy disengaged, much to the relief of his son and daughter. "Well, what are we waiting for, gang? Let's check it out!"

When they entered the front entrance, they found the narrow building crammed with all manner of Tennessee souvenirs and spider-related merchandise. To the left was a small snack bar with four stools and, behind it, a teenage boy who couldn't have been older than sixteen or seventeen. To the right were the restrooms. Rough barnwood boards had been Gorilla Glued to the doors, making them look like outhouse doors. Each was identified by gender… either Ma or Pa.

"Welcome, folks!" called a tall, jovial man behind the counter at the very back of the building. He had a graying crewcut, a bushy beard that needed trimming, and wore a bright blue Hawaiian shirt decorated with cobwebs and black widows. "Just in time for the two o'clock tour. Step right up and buy your tickets here!'

Joe purchased four admissions, which came to forty bucks even. He grinned at Brandon and gave his son a high-five. Cindy and Lacey stood there, arms crossed, looking like they would rather be anywhere else in the world but where they stood at that moment.

Set into the wall beside the admission counter, behind a chain barrier, was a stainless-steel elevator door. Perched on a stool next to the elevator was a pretty, blond girl that was probably the same age as the snack bar boy. She wore a khaki shirt and shorts, and wore a baseball cap with a rubber tarantula glued to the crown.

Come See Spider Cave!

Embroidered across the front of the cap was OFFICIAL SPIDER CAVE TOUR GUIDE.

There were two other people waiting for the tour to begin; an elderly man and woman in their mid-seventies… the owners of the Airstream, no doubt. "Folks, this is Earl and Sylvia Goldstein of York, Pennsylvania," said the extroverted proprietor of the attraction. "They'll be joining you on the tour. And I'm the owner of the World-Famous Spider Cave, Big Mike Winfree. Your tour guide this afternoon will be the lovely Susan Grace here. She's only been working with us a week now, but she's knowledgeable in spider facts and lore… and not afraid of the dark. And, following your subterranean experience, you can grab yourself a snack over where my son, Johnny, is standing yonder. Say hi to the folks, son."

They looked over at the snack bar. The pimply boy waved indifferently and wiped down the eating counter with a wet rag. His attention seemed to be directed more at the pretty girl on the stool than his father's afternoon customers.

Big Mike glanced up at a clock on the wall. "We'll wait just a few more minutes… in case more *victims* arrive." He winked at Brandon, drawing a big grin from the boy. "You know, they used to come by the busloads before the interstate took the traffic a dozen miles east. In the thirties and forties, this place was the biggest tourist attraction between Knoxville and Atlanta. Of course, the elevator was pretty primitive back then. We installed a brand new one in back in '84. Wouldn't want anyone to get stuck down there with all those nasty, eight-legged critters!"

Joe felt someone tug gently on his hand. He looked down at his daughter.

Lacey was mouthing *Let's get out of here, Dad… please?* He smiled at her silent plea, tousled her golden hair, and turned back toward their host. "When I was kid, there was an old man here…"

"That would have been my father-in-law, Jasper Knowles. He ran this place for pert near fifty years, until his death in 2007. His father, Hezekiah Knowles, discovered the cave way back in 1921. He was what you might call a spelunker. If there was a hole in the earth or a cave in a hillside, he had to know where it led to and what was inside it. In this case, it was the biggest spider-infested cavern in the South."

Cindy couldn't help but shudder. It was that one word that triggered the response. *Infested.*

After five minutes, Big Mike decided that no one else was going to show up, so he stepped to the side and unclasped the length of chain. "Step this way, ladies and gentlemen, and the most fascinating and exciting tour of your lives will now begin!"

The blond girl named Susan Grace hopped off her stool and pressed a button in a panel on the wall. There was a noisy clang and clatter as the elevator roared into life and, after a moment, the steel doors opened, revealing a cramped car with handrails long the walls. Someone had decorated the ceiling of the elevator with Halloween cobwebs and plastic spiders for added effect.

"Y'all step right this way," the girl invited with an infectious smile, as she collected tickets from the six passengers. Soon, they all stood within the cubicle, shoulder to shoulder. Joe, Brandon, and Earl Goldstein were grinning from ear to ear, while Cindy, Lacey, and Silvia looked like they wanted to cut and run, leaving their men to explore the depths of Spider Cave alone. But, despite their reluctance, they stood rooted to the spot.

"See y'all in a little while," Big Mike told them, pressing the DOWN button from where he stood behind the counter. "Hopefully!"

A minute later, the seven occupants were descending into the cavern's only access passage… a shaft that dropped a thousand feet straight down into the earth. Several times, the car lurched and shuddered, drawing gasps and giggles. "Don't worry, folks," Susan Grace told them. "We haven't lost an explorer yet." Her teeth, all ivory and silver braces, beamed brilliantly in the gloom of the car,

Come See Spider Cave!

while her eyes seemed a tad uneasy. At least to Cindy they seemed that way.

Finally, they reached the bottom of the shaft. With the ding of a bell, the elevator doors opened. Beyond were the smooth, stone walls of a cave, illuminated by a string of sixty-watt light bulbs dangling overhead.

"Please exit the car and we shall proceed with the tour." Susan Grace moved her pale hands in a practiced flourish, looking much like a Subterranean Barbie. The Stanton family and the Goldsteins did as she instructed and, soon, they were all standing in a narrow chamber. They watched as the girl pressed a button next to the door that read UP. Next to it was a bright red plastic button that was marked ALARM. With a hiss, the elevator doors closed and they could hear the car rattling and bumping as it returned to the surface.

"Now, if you'll follow me to the left, we will..."

"Pardon me, miss," said Joe Stanton, looking off toward the right. "Wasn't this tunnel blocked before? I remember when I was a kid, there was a wall of stalactites and stalagmites grown together... sort of like the bars of a jail cell. I believe the old man called it the Hoosegow."

"Yes, I've been told there was something like that there." She looked off into the dark tunnel that yawned beyond a bright red border line that had been painted across the cave floor. Was that a hint of *fear* that showed in her pretty, blue eyes? "There was a mild earthquake a few years ago that damaged the formations, so Big Mike had the debris cleared away."

"Sure looks creepy!" said Brandon, taking a step in that direction.

"It's off limits to visitors, though," said Susan Grace, a little too quickly, stepping to block the boy's way. "Now if you will all turn to your left, we will begin our exciting journey to Spider Cave."

They did as they were told, following her in single file. For a while, the bulbs overhead lit the way. But a couple of hundred feet further on, the lights ended and only darkness yawned before them. Susan Grace produced a halogen flashlight that hung on her belt and snapped it on. The circle of light was bright enough to reach fifty feet or so down the passageway.

As they followed their guide, Brandon spoke up. "Are there any bats in this cave?"

"If there were," Susan Grace told him, "they've already been eaten by the spiders."

The men laughed at the joke, while the woman found no humor in the statement whatsoever. The girl pointed out interesting cave formations as they strolled along the narrow corridor; outcroppings that resembled a crowing rooster, a slab of bacon, an elephant's foot.

"We have finally reached our destination," she said, lowering her voice. "Please, I must ask that you be as quiet as possible. The spiders that call this cavern their home are shy and skittish. We must respect the fact that this is *their* home and that we are only visitors in their domain. Does everyone understand?"

The six nodded in agreement.

"Stand right here until I tell you to proceed." The teenager walked a couple of yards further and stepped into a natural doorway in the cave wall, peaked like the entrance of a cathedral. She stooped down and tripped a number of toggle switches in a steel box on the floor. Instantly, klieg lights lit up, bathing the cavern beyond in brilliant yellow light.

She turned and waved for them to proceed. "Ladies and Gentlemen, I present to you… the World-Renowned… the One and Only… SPIDER CAVE!"

The six moved slowly forward and passed through the arched doorway. What they witnessed beyond the portal was truly an awe-inspiring sight to behold.

Come See Spider Cave!

The klieg lights revealed a massive cavern that was two hundred feet deep, a hundred feet wide, and a good seventy-five feet in height. Sharp stalactites hung from the ceiling like layered fangs and, draped from one to the other, were great sheets of webbing. That, in itself, was impressive... almost a thing of beauty... with the sparkle and shine of quartz and gypsum adding to the silky luminance of the artificial light upon the network of interlacing cobwebs.

But what amazed them the most were the spiders. Not one or two species, but every kind imaginable. Black widow, brown recluse, tarantula, trap door, wolf, garden, hobo, spiney orb weaver, even King Baboon and Goliath Bird-eaters. Not only were many totally out of their element or places of origin, but they weren't normal in size. They weren't only oversized or even big... but unnervingly *huge*

"I don't think I've ever seen spiders this big before," muttered Earl Goldstein, eying a black widow as big as his hand.

"I don't like this," Cindy whispered to her husband. "It's... it's *unnatural.*" She cringed at the sight of a tarantula so large that it could have embraced a man's head and smothered him.

"It's cool as hell, is what it is," Joe told her, gazing at the thousands upon thousands of subterranean arachnids that skittered and crept across the gleaming webs.

Brandon's freckled face held something akin to rapture. "Yeah," he said softly. "Cool as hell."

"Don't curse, Brand," his mom scolded half-heartedly. She looked over at Susan Grace. "Miss, is this all there is to see?"

"Uh... yes, ma'am. This is it. This is Spider Cave."

"Then could we cut this visit short and get back upstairs?" Cindy held Lacey tightly to her side. "I believe this is starting to frighten my daughter." The eight-year-old girl's eyes were wide and startled as she clung to her mother's hip.

"I second that motion," said matronly Sylvia Goldstein. They suddenly realized that the elderly woman's eyes had pretty much been closed the entire time they had stood in the cavern.

"Oh... yes, I'm sorry. " Susan Grace cleared her throat. "If you will please follow me, we shall proceed back down the outer corridor to our starting point at the elevator."

Brandon groaned. "Aw, man! Do we have to go this soon?"

"Maybe we can come back sometimes," his father suggested.

Cindy turned and nailed Joe with a withering glare. *Not on your life, mister!*

Fifteen minutes later, they were back at the elevator. "I hope you all enjoyed your exploration of the World-Famous Spider Cave," the girl said. "We will now enter the elevator and return to the surface. Remember to shop for all our frightfully spidery souvenirs and satisfy your culinary cravings at our four-star snack bar. Take it from me, Johnny can make a delicious banana split or order of chili cheese fries."

Susan Grace pushed the UP button. They all waited patiently as the sound of the car could be heard, descending to the floor of the shaft. Two hundred feet, four hundred. Then, abruptly, there was a shrill squeal of seized rotors and a jarring clash of steel against steel somewhere from above. Then total silence.

They looked toward the teenager. She frowned and jabbed her finger at the control button again. There was another squeal, then a creak, and a violent thump as the car shuddered and stopped. Susan Grace laughed nervously. "Uh... it gets stuck sometimes."

"Let me give it a try," suggested Earl Goldstein. He pressed the button firmly with the ball of his thumb. But nothing happened. There was no sound of machinery at all.

Somewhere, in the darkness to their right, came an echo.

"What was that?" asked Lacey.

"Don't worry, sweetheart," their guide said, trying to sound encouraging, but failing miserably. "I'll just push the alarm and Big

Come See Spider Cave!

Mike and Johnny will have the elevator working, good as new, in no time."

Again, a sound from the tunnel to their right... where the formation known as the Hoosegow had once blocked the passageway. A scratching, scrabbling noise.

Susan Grace's eyes darted toward the tunnel as her thumb pressed the bright red button. Somewhere above, the jangle of an alarm went off. It sounded like it was a thousand miles away, instead of a thousand feet.

More skittering... scrabbling... scratching. Something moving along shadowy cave walls... across the smooth stone floor. To their right.

Cindy held Lacey tightly against her. She reached out for Brandon. The boy, pale-faced and frightened, went to his mother willingly. "Joe?"

Joe peered into the dark corridor as the sound grew louder. Nearer.

"Miss?"

"It's fine," mumbled the girl. "The bell is ringing... help is on the way."

"Oh, dear *God*," moaned Earl. Sylvia moved quickly behind her husband, using him as a shield, burrowing her face against his back.

Joe pushed Cindy and the kids behind him and peered into the tunnel. The darkness of the tunnel grew darker in places. Along the walls... across the jagged spires that hung from the ceiling. The tip of a shadow moved across the red line painted on the tunnel floor. It stretched forward... long, lean, and hairy. Hinged in the middle... moving stealthily. Skittering... scrambling.

Joe's heart pounded. He turned toward the girl who had brought them down to Spider Cave. "Miss?"

Tears bloomed in Susan Grace's eyes as she pounded the red button again and again and again.

"Come on… come on… please… *please*.. come on!

Somewhere above them the alarm sounded. Long and loud. Time and time again.

But no one seemed to answer.

An hour later, the innerworkings of the elevator machinery roared into life and it descended slowly. Foot by foot… yard by yard.

The door opened with a cheerful *ding*. Big Mike stood there, grimly. Grease blackened his face and arms, and stained the spider pattern of his silk shirt. In his hands, he held a twelve-gauge shotgun.

Working the pump, he stepped into the chamber beyond the lift. Johnny followed, holding a revolver in his hand. Like the scattergun, it was a big bore… forty-four caliber. Anything less would have been downright foolish… and useless.

The first thing they looked at was the floor. What they saw there was awful… but not unexpected.

A child's sneaker. A purse torn in half. A man's broken eyeglasses. And a bloody baseball cap with a rubber spider sewed to the top.

Johnny moaned. "You never should've done it, Daddy. Never should've took that sledgehammer and knocked down the Hoosegow." He recalled how his father had put it. *To expand the business.*

"Hush, boy," Big Mike said, as softly as he could manage. "I admit that was a bad move… but that's water under the bridge. Ain't nothing to be done to fix it."

Come See Spider Cave!

The teenager heard something in the distance... somewhere off down the tunnel... in the darkness. A whimper. Soft, pitiful, hopeless.

"Susan Grace?" Johnny called out, although he couldn't have told if the sound had come from a male or female, adult or child.

Big Mike slapped his son across the shoulder. "I said to shut up!" he hissed. "Now let's get this over and done with."

Johnny took a garbage bag from his hip pocket and, together, they began to gather what was scattered across the floor. Soon, nothing was left. Nothing but a few splatters and pockets of blood on the uneven stone.

"We'll come back later with a couple of buckets and swill down the place," his father told him. "Let it dry a couple of days, before we reopen."

"Reopen," the boy said dully. "But, Daddy..."

Something moved way back in the tunnel. Scrambling... skittering.

Something big.

Big Mike shoved his son back into the elevator and, taking the garbage bag with them, pressed the inner button. With a lurch, the six-by-six chamber lifted upward, heading toward ground level.

The man paced back and forth, mulling things over in his mind. "I'll have your uncle come tonight... after dark... and tow the van and truck to his junkyard. The camper... damn, I wanna sell it bad, but we may have to rip it apart and burn it. Can't leave any trace... that they were ever here."

"Like last time," said the boy, standing tightly in a back corner of the elevator. "And the time before last."

"Now, listen to me, Johnny." Big Mike thought about it for a moment, choosing his words carefully. "I promised your mama... promised her on her deathbed that her papa's and grandpapa's legacy would live on. That Spider Cave wouldn't be shut down and forgotten. Don't worry none... we'll get this elevator motor rebuilt… the cables replaced… the pulleys oiled, running smooth as owl grease. Just you wait and see."

"How many times are you going to promise that, Daddy?" Tears ran down the boy's pimpled cheeks. "How many?" He recalled the whimper in the dark. "Oh God… Susan…"

Roughly, Big Mike grabbed the boy by the chin, lifting his eyes to meet his own. "Man up, son! You know what's got to be done to keep this place open… to keep it alive." He released his grip on the young man's jaw and patted him gently on the cheek. "Just remember…all this will be yours someday."

Johnny had no doubt. He knew that his father was right.

That was what scared him the most.

About the Author

Ronald Kelly began his writing career in 1986 and quickly sold his first short story, "Breakfast Serial," to *Terror Time Again* magazine. His first novel, *Hindsight*, was released by Zebra Books in 1990. His audiobook collection, *Dark Dixie: Tales of Southern Horror*, was on the nominating ballot of the 1992 Grammy Awards for Best Spoken Word or Non-Musical Album. Zebra published seven of Ronald Kelly's novels from 1990 to 1996. Ronald's short fiction work has been published by *Cemetery Dance*, *Borderlands 3*, *Deathrealm*, *Dark at Heart*, *Hot Blood: Seeds of Fear*, and many more. After selling hundreds of thousands of books, the bottom dropped out of the horror market in 1996. So, when Zebra dropped their horror line in October 1996, Ronald Kelly stopped writing for almost ten years and worked various jobs including welder, factory worker, production manager, drugstore manager, and custodian.

In 2006, Ronald Kelly started writing again. Since then, he has written and published several new novels (*Hell Hollow*, *Restless Shadows*, and *The Buzzard Zone*), numerous short story collections, and has become an elder statesman of Southern-Fried Horror in his chosen genre. In 2021, his collection of extreme horror tales, *The Essential Sick Stuff*, won the Splatterpunk Award for Best Collection. He is currently working on The Saga of Dead-Eye, a five-volume horror western series.

Ronald Kelly currently lives in a backwoods hollow in Brush Creek, Tennessee, with his wife and young'uns.

Book List

Novels
Blood Kin
Father's Little Helper (re-released as Twelve Gauge)
Fear
Fear Eternal (forthcoming)
Hell Hollow
Hindsight
Moon of the Werewolf (re-released as Undertaker's Moon)
Pitfall
Restless Shadows
Something Out There (re-released as The Dark'Un)
The Buzzard Zone
The China Doll
The Possession (re-released as Burnt Magnolia)
The Saga of Dead-Eye, Book One:
    Vampires, Zombies, & Mojo Men
The Saga of Dead-Eye, Book Two:
    Werewolves, Swamp Critters, & Hellacious Haints
The Saga of Dead-Eye, Book Three:
    Man-Eaters, Mummies, & Murderous Maniacs
The Saga of Dead-Eye, Book Four:
    Golems, Ghouls, & Grisly Gargantuans
Timber Gray

Novellas
Flesh Welder

Collections
After the Burn
Cumberland Furnace and Other Fear Forged Fables
Dark Dixie
Dark Dixie II

Haunt of Southern-Fried Fear
Irish Gothic: Tales of Celtic Horror
Long Chills
Midnight Tide & Other Seaside Stories
Mister Glow-Bones & Other Halloween Tales
More Sick Stuff
Season's Creepings: Tales of Holiday Horror
Tales from the Southern-Fried Crypt
The Essential Sick Stuff
The Halloween Store and Other Tales of All Hallows' Eve
The Shrouded Tome: Ten Forgotten Fables
The Sick Stuff
The Web of La Sanguinaire and Other Arachnid Horrors
Twilight Hankerings
Unhinged
Vault of Southern-Fried Horror

Curious about other Crossroad Press books? Stop by our
website: http://crossroadpress.com
We offer quality writing
in digital, audio, and print formats.

Subscribe to our newsletter on the website homepage and receive
a free eBook.

www.ingramcontent.com/pod-product-compliance
Lightning Source LLC